*Samuel French Acting Edition*

# The Men From T̶h̶e̶ ̶B̶o̶y̶s̶

A Sequel

*by* Mart Crowley

# SAMUEL FRENCH

SAMUELFRENCH.COM   SAMUELFRENCH.CO.UK

Copyright © 2004 by Mart Crowley
All Rights Reserved

*THE MEN FROM THE BOYS* is fully protected under the copyright laws of the United States of America, the British Commonwealth, including Canada, and all other countries of the Copyright Union. All rights, including professional and amateur stage productions, recitation, lecturing, public reading, motion picture, radio broadcasting, television and the rights of translation into foreign languages are strictly reserved.

ISBN 978-0-573-62906-8

www.SamuelFrench.com
www.SamuelFrench.co.uk

---

### For Production Enquiries

**United States and Canada**
Info@SamuelFrench.com
1-866-598-8449

**United Kingdom and Europe**
Plays@SamuelFrench.co.uk
020-7255-4302

Each title is subject to availability from Samuel French, depending upon country of performance. Please be aware that *THE MEN FROM THE BOYS* may not be licensed by Samuel French in your territory. Professional and amateur producers should contact the nearest Samuel French office or licensing partner to verify availability.

---

CAUTION: Professional and amateur producers are hereby warned that *THE MEN FROM THE BOYS* is subject to a licensing fee. Publication of this play(s) does not imply availability for performance. Both amateurs and professionals considering a production are strongly advised to apply to Samuel French before starting rehearsals, advertising, or booking a theatre. A licensing fee must be paid whether the title(s) is presented for charity or gain and whether or not admission is charged. Professional/Stock licensing fees are quoted upon application to Samuel French.

No one shall make any changes in this title(s) for the purpose of production. No part of this book may be reproduced, stored in a retrieval system, or transmitted in any form, by any means, now known or yet to be invented, including mechanical, electronic, photocopying, recording, videotaping, or otherwise, without the prior written permission of the publisher. No one shall upload this title(s), or part of this title(s), to any social media websites.

For all enquiries regarding motion picture, television, and other media rights, please contact Samuel French.

## MUSIC USE NOTE

Licensees are solely responsible for obtaining formal written permission from copyright owners to use copyrighted music in the performance of this play and are strongly cautioned to do so. If no such permission is obtained by the licensee, then the licensee must use only original music that the licensee owns and controls. Licensees are solely responsible and liable for all music clearances and shall indemnify the copyright owners of the play(s) and their licensing agent, Samuel French, against any costs, expenses, losses and liabilities arising from the use of music by licensees. Please contact the appropriate music licensing authority in your territory for the rights to any incidental music.

## IMPORTANT BILLING AND CREDIT REQUIREMENTS

If you have obtained performance rights to this title, please refer to your licensing agreement for important billing and credit requirements.

### *The Men From the Boys*
### *by Mart Crowley*

had its World Premiere on October 26, 2002 at the New Conservatory Theatre Center, San Francisco, California, Ed Decker, Artistic Director. The scene design was by Eric Sinkkonen, the music by Larry Grossman, and the stage manager was Phillip Lienau. The play was produced and directed by Mr. Decker.

The cast was:

| | |
|---|---|
| Donald | Peter Carlstrom |
| Michael | Russ Duffy |
| Emory | Michael Patrick Gaffney |
| Scott | Olen Christian Holm |
| Harold | Will Huddleston |
| Hank | Terry Lamb |
| Rick | Rajiv Shah |
| Bernard | Lewis Sims |
| Jason | Owen Thomas |

*Special thanks to:*

Andrew Nance
(Actor, Conservatory Director)

Buddy Thomas
(Playwright, Agent
who brought TMFTB to TNCTC)

Keri Fitch (Costumes), Melissa Kalstrom (Wigs, Hair and Makeup),
Victoria Kirby (Publicity), Nancy Mancias (Properties),
Jonathan Retsky (Lighting), and Steve Romanko (Sound Design).

*NCTC and the author wish to acknowledge*

Mr. Steven Buss
*and also*
Mr. Arnold Stiefel
Of Stiefel Entertainment

for their individual support and generosity.

---

THE MEN FROM THE BOYS
*has been selected as a 2004 Lambda Literary Award Nominee*

## CHARACTERS

MICHAEL: 59, a comb-over, well groomed.
DONALD: 57, trim, ageing boy-next door.
EMORY: 62, pink, plump.
HANK: 61, distinguished.
BERNARD: 57, African American, good-looking.
SCOTT: 26, a beauty.
JASON: 33, pumped-up, sexy
RICK: 24, Asian American, cute.
HAROLD: 61, thin, pock-marked.

## ACT I

*THE SET: A deliberate reproduction of the concept for an East 50's Manhattan duplex (bedroom upstairs), designed by Peter Harvey for* THE BOYS IN THE BAND: *a black-and-white photo blow-up collage of chic rooms (as seen in interior décor magazines), which completely covers all wall surfaces. Abstract and stylish.*
*In the original production there were only "Deco" black Naugahyde chairs, a settee and a couple of chrome and glass side tables. That was it. In any case, the effect should be deliberately minimal, monochromatic and clean-lined without a single unnecessary item of dressing. Dramatic and anal. And, of course, it should positively scream "taste."*
*From a state of complete darkness the lights suddenly illuminate full-tilt to reveal a stage occupied by five characters from TBITB, now thirty years older but still pulled-together. Their ages (and the state of their hair) are: MICHAEL, fifty-nine, thin-ish, or a meticulous, studied comb-over; EMORY, sixty-two, dyed auburn; BERNARD, fifty-seven, salt and pepper; DONALD, fifty-seven, blond/silver; and HANK, sixty-one, distinguished gray temples. HAROLD, sixty-one, with receding curly black hair, will enter eventually.*
*This quintet is positioned formally at various interesting levels: standing with hands in pockets or arms folded; seated on a chair or a stool or the stairs. They all look directly at the audience, completely poker-faced (sad? dazed? imperious?), as if caught in an artfully composed still of the early Avedon/Stern school. All wear suits or jackets and ties: EMORY in a Charvet bow cravat*

*and black velour suit (minus the jacket); MICHAEL in a charcoal gray flannel two-piece Armani and solid charcoal tie. DONALD, has loosened his striped rep, unfastened his button-down collar and removed his navy Brooks Brothers blazer to sling it over his shoulder.*

*The "men" of the title are lit in hotter pools of light than three new "boys," who face upstage with their backs to the audience. They are SCOTT, twenty-six, JASON, a thirty-something, both Caucasians; and RICK, twenty-four, an Asian-American. They are all dressed in more relaxed, up-to-the-minute styles from slacks and pullovers to jeans and jackets with T-shirts. They are scattered among the originals, posed in more casual attitudes: draped against the stairs, lolling on the back of the sofa or lying on the floor, propped on an arm. Their facial attitudes are concealed, but their body language varies from studied casual to subtly provocative.*

*After the "shock illumination" of the frieze, there is what seems to be an* interminable *pause. We hear only the sound of heavy rain and EMORY's delicately pulling a needle and yarn through a small, unfinished petit point pattern. The dimmer circles of light sneak to the level of the hotter ones. No one moves or speaks. The older characters continue to stare straight forward, enigmatic; the younger ones remain turned-away, their attitudes unknown. Then, just as the audience is about to break with restless nervousness, in reaction to the prolonged silence, stillness and scrutiny, EMORY starts to cough uncontrollably. Everyone else slowly, deliberately turns his head without moving his body to glare at EMORY (disapprovingly? sympathetically? affectlessly?) and hold until EMORY calms, heavily clears his throat.*

*—Finally, EMORY sheepishly scans the sea of attention, chagrined at everyone looking at him ....*

EMORY. *(Tongue-in-cheek.)* — It must be the excitement. — We're having too much fun here.

*(No one cracks a smile. Not a titter. They all continue to look at EMORY a moment longer (contempt? compassion? indifference?), then DONALD breaks the mood, flings his blazer aside, goes to a drinks cart and pours a crystal tumbler of water from a pitcher.)*

MICHAEL. *(Sardonically.)* Excitement, indeed! Some "celebration of life"! It's so fucking quite in here, you could hear boll weevils pissing on cotton!

DONALD. *(Palm to ear.)* Listen! I think I hear them! — No, it's just pissing with rain.

MICHAEL. Let's have some music, Bernard. Liven-up this taffy-pull.

BERNARD. *(Facetiously.)* Sure. I'll just put on a little gangsta rap.

*(BERNARD goes to an étagère, begins to shuffle through some CDs.)*

MICHAEL. *(Dryly, offhand.)* You do and there's gonna be some strange fruit hangin' from the poplar trees.

*(EMORY, with an arched "Ahem!" clears his throat at MICHAEL's "wit." RICK, the exotically attractive Asian-American, speaks up ...)*

RICK. *(To MICHAEL.)* Is that a racist remark?

BERNARD. *(Weary, tongue-in-cheek.)* — Well, Michael's not exactly out in a cornfield at midnight, burning crosses. His ambivalent generation of so-called Southern liberals has just got to *die*-out, before its tacit gut feelings are completely extinct. *(Dryly.)* — It shouldn't be too long now.

*(Meanwhile, DONALD has crossed to EMORY, hands him a tumbler.)*

DONALD. — Here, Emory, drink some water.

EMORY. Is it bottled or just from the tap?
MICHAEL. *(Quickly, on edge.)* It's from the toilet. It's toilet water. Every morning I submerge an empty Evian bottle in the toilet. It's multipurpose eau de toilette — you can either drink it or put it behind your ears.

*(EMORY shoots MICHAEL a withering look, takes a sip from the tumbler, returns it to DONALD.)*

EMORY. *(Sweetly.)* Thanks, Donald. You're a real sis'.

*(This remark is met with some audible groans from JASON, BERNARD and DONALD. (Note: There is an open bottle of Dom Perignon in a wine cooler on the cart and HANK and RICK each take a sip of champagne from flutes already in their hands.)*
*Everyone begins to shift, get up and move about. All except SCOTT, the loner with the knockout good looks, who noticeably remains apart from the group — perhaps leaning on the far side of the stairs, hands in pockets, staring into space.)*

BARNARD. *(Generally, re: EMORY.)* Wouldn't you know she only drinks designer water.
EMORY. Don't say "she"! You, of all people, know that's *not* politically correct! *(Big flirty smile to JASON.)* — Is it, Jason? —
BERNARD. *(Quickly, to EMORY.)* Calling people "sis" is not exactly *enlightened*.

*(JASON, proletariat activist, gym-body, sexy in an obvious way, turns at the mention of his name....)*

JASON. It's all right, Emory. We make allowances for those who have gone before.
EMORY. *(Drawing himself up.)* Do I detect the remotest innuendo that I am slightly older than you?

## THE MEN FROM THE BOYS

JASON. *(To EMORY.)* You planted the redwoods, didn't you?

*(Some scattered laughter. EMORY makes a quick decision to take the high road....)*

EMORY. *(To JASON, mock-insulted.)* Oh, you're *terrible!* (Coy, a beat.) — But I like you.

*(JASON looks indifferent, turns away. EMORY recovers with a certain practiced (and practical) dignity, joins BERNARD at the étagère to select CDs.)*

DONALD. Did you know the U.N. declared this "The Year of the Older Person"?
JASON. I'm glad they *declared* something.
MICHAEL. *(Still on earlier thought.)* — I *am* the most liberal Confederate who ever lived! Why, when I was sixteen my father gave me a convertible, and do you know my best friend was a black gay boy. — Oh, he'd have to sit in the back seat, of course, so no one would say anything. It was the acceptable, hypocritical, *idiotic* way things were done.
BERNARD. If you'd had any guts, you'd have made him sit in the front.
MICHAEL. Then he'd have looked like the chauffeur.
BERNARD. In the *passenger* seat *beside* you!
MICHAEL. Funny thing, Bernard, dear. Neither of us wanted our balls between a split rail. We were smart. *We played the system.*
JASON. Somebody has to put their balls on the line sometime.
MICHAEL. *(Re: empty flutes.)* Jason, why don't you *act-up* like the old days and freshen everyone's drinks. You're so good at it.
JASON. That's why I'm a bartender *these* days — on my *working hours.*
MICHAEL. Oh, well, if you're offended and going to picket or protest this solemn occasion then ....

*(JASON ignores MICHAEL, goes to the bar cart as RICK, the young Asian-American, speaks....)*

RICK. *(To EMORY.)* You're the first real interior decorator I've ever been around.

EMORY. Designer. We prefer interior *designer*. Like flight attendants prefer "flight attendant" instead of "stewardess."

JASON. Or "steward," if you happen to be a man.

EMORY. *(Quick and pointed.)* So few are.

BERNARD. *(To JASON.)* You've had more careers that anybody I know.

JASON. *(Refills his flute.)* Mmm, I've careered from career to career, to quote somebody, and guess what? —

MICHAEL. You're still queer.

JASON. I'm still a major fuck-up.

DONALD. *(Crosses to JASON.)* I thought *I* held that title.

JASON. Just can't seem to find my calling.

BERNARD. Why *not* go into politics? Being a fuck-up seems to be a prerequisite.

JASON. *I'm* too old for that. Haven't got a law degree and haven't got the money to get one. Had to drop out, as it was. *(To DONALD.)* — What can I do for you, sir?

DONALD. *(Bit too flirtatious.)* Beer. — No, a glass of wine. — No, an extra dry Bombay martini on the rocks, please?

EMORY. Beer!-Wine!-Booze! Make up your mind! It's readiness that makes a woman!

JASON. — More champagne, Hank?

HANK. No, thanks.

JASON. *(Re: empty bucket.)* We need ice. —

MICHAEL. There's no ice? — I thought ….

DONALD. *(Picks up bucket.)* I'll get it.

SCOTT. — *I'll* get it. — Sorry.

*(DONALD stops. Everyone reacts to SCOTT having spoken. He goes*

*to DONALD, takes the silver ice bucket.)*

DONALD. *(To SCOTT.)* You don't mind doing it?
SCOTT. *(For MICHAEL's benefit.)* I'll do anything if I'm not humiliated.
MICHAEL. *(To SCOTT, calmly, seriously.)* Did I humiliate you? — Have I *ever* humiliated you? *(No answer.)* — Well? — *(SCOTT exits off left to kitchen.)* — I guess that was a rhetorical question.
EMORY. *(CDs in hand.)* — So, what are we going to do, kids? Put on some music and dance our tits off?
DONALD. *(Moving away.)* I'd rather be in a ditch.
EMORY. *(Ever the fun one.)* Well, then, I just heard about this marvelous new party game! Everyone takes his clothes off and forms two parallel lines, facing each other. And then, when someone yells, "Go!" the two lines make a mad stampede toward each other ... and the first one that get in gets a kiss! *(He breaks himself up, laughing. Nobody else cracks a smile, just glares at him again. Trying to save the moment.)* I forgot to say condoms are passed out first. — Does that it make it funnier? *(Silence.)* — Okay, why don't we all just pull on our wetsuits and grovel around on top of each other?
MICHAEL. *(Grimly, calmly.)* — There will be no dancing. There will be no games played. And for the duration of this event, no one is allowed to take off so much as a necktie. For that, you'll have to see some *serious* gay theatre. All-male nude Chekhov, that sort of thing.
BERNARD. *(To EMORY.)* No nudity tonight. Not with *this* crowd. *(Looks at JASON.)* — Well, not with *most* of this crowd.
RICK. *(Re: earlier thought.)* I'm glad we're not gonna play that game!
EMORY. *(To RICK, sympathy.)* Me, too, actually. Because of a few unwanted kilos. But, I'll soon have a new bod. I now have a personal trainer and he's marvelous. — He said to me, "First we lose the weight, then we sculpt."
BERNARD. That ought to be as simple as chopping a fifth face

on Mount Rushmore.
EMORY. I've lost four pounds! Can't you tell?
DONALD. Not from *this* angle.
BERNARD. *(Re: music.)* Whatta you want, Michael? *(Quickly.)* — EllaMabelJudyPeggyBarbara — or Bobby?
MICHAEL. You know I won't own any Streisand.
EMORY. *(Holding up a CD.)* Yes, you do, right here, The Second Album, the one that's got "When in Rome" on it.
MICHAEL. That belongs to Harold.
JASON. Is there anything that was written in the last forty years? *(MICHAEL gives JASON a look as SCOTT enters with the filled bucket. BERNARD puts on Chet Baker's recording of "Tenderly"\* or a similar style recording. To SCOTT, taking bucket.)* Thanks, Scott. — What'll it be?
SCOTT. *(Dryly.)* I'll have some of that toilet water. With a twist.

*(JASON puts some ice in the martini he has made, hands it to DONALD.)*

JASON. Donald. —
DONALD. Thanks. — *(JASON pours SCOTT an Evian water. SCOTT returns to the outer limits by the stairs. DONALD sips drink, reacts.)* Oh, yeah, Jason, that's good.
JASON. *(Smiles noncommittally.)* Thank you sir. —

*(JASON walks away from the drinks cart with a can of Diet Coke just as EMORY says ...)*

EMORY. I'd like some coffee. —

*(JASON pops the top of the Diet Coke can and drinks. EMORY forces a stiff smile at being ignored. RICK puts down his drink, picks up*

---

\*References to recordings or songs in this acting edition do not constitute permission to use the song(s) in your production. Synchronization rights for use of any music within the production must be obtained from the copyright holder.

**THE MEN FROM THE BOYS** 15

*a silver coffeepot and cup and saucer from the drinks cart.)*

RICK. *(Pleasantly, to EMORY re: coffee.)* How do you like it?
EMORY. *(Campily sultry.)* Like I like my men.
BERNARD. *(To EMORY, re: RICK.)* Sorry, he ain't got no gay coffee!
EMORY. *(Snaps.)* I meant hot and café au lait!
BERNARD. He knows what you meant. And he still doesn't give a shit.

*(EMORY sucks a tooth, nose in the air. SCOTT and MICHAEL exchange a look at the mention of "English" and "school." SCOTT turns away. RICK picks up the silver coffeepot, looks at it appreciatively.)*

RICK. *(Ingenuously, not a trace of chichi.)* What a nice coffeepot. — Nice and simple, you know.

*(RICK pours EMORY a cup....)*

EMORY. And a lovely ice bucket too. Really too lovely for ice. *(To MICHAEL.)* You ought to float a pansy in it.
MICHAEL. *("Menacingly.")* I might just do that. Facedown.

*(RICK hands the coffee to Emory....)*

RICK. *(Pleasantly.)* There you go, Emory. —
EMORY. *(Taking the cup, with flirty charm.)* Merci, mille fois.
RICK. *(Innocently.)* Oh, you speak French?
EMORY. No, I was just …. Well, it's hard to explain exactly. It's what used to be called *charm.* — Of course, that was a while back. — *(A look to JASON.)* Only those who've "gone before" might remember.
RICK. *(Back a beat, to EMORY.)* — I just thought with a name

like Em-or-*ee* ... and café au lait ... *(Re: MICHAEL.)* and him saying the thing about Evi*an (French pronunciation of Evian: "Aye-vee-anh.")* ... and ....

MICHAEL. *(Tolerantly.)* I have a name, too, and it's not *him*, it's Michael.

RICK. *(Conciliatory.)* — Sorry. *(Continuing to EMORY.)* — And *Michael* here, saying the thing about ... well, I don't know, I just thought you might be French or something. — Cause *I* speak French.

*(EMORY is silent, thinking this over.)*

MICHAEL. *(To EMORY.)* Did you follow that? Or were you knocked senseless by *The Great Language Barrier Reef of Time?*

EMORY. *(To RICK, simply.)* Emory was my mother's family name and she wasn't French. — At least, if she was she never told *me*.

RICK. My mother *was* French. Well, French-Vietnamese.

MICHAEL. *(To RICK, slightly grand.)* — I don't believe we've been formally introduced. —

RICK. *(Extends his hand.)* Oh, I should have introduced myself.

MICHAEL. — I mean, you *look* familiar, but ....

RICK. *(Shakes hands with MICHAEL.)* I'm out of uniform.

*(MICHAEL reacts oddly, takes this in.)*

HANK. *(To RICK.)* Well, *I* know you. — I remember you nights — mostly nights.

RICK. *(To MICHAEL.)* — Yeah, the graveyard shift. I'm a practical nurse. Part time.

MICHAEL. Oh, of course, you are!

RICK. *(Tentatively.)* — When Larry couldn't sleep, we'd talk — or I'd just hold his hand. We ... became quite close. — He gave me some of his artwork ... stuff he had in his room. And some books. *(To HANK.)* — I hope you don't mind.

HANK. Why should I? They were his things.

RICK. *(To MICHAEL.)* — I know I wasn't exactly invited, but I thought it was kind of an open house ....

MICHAEL. *(Chagrined.)* Oh, it is. — Why, you're *very, very* welcome, Rick. I just don't remember you. I wasn't there much in the evening, but, then, Larry tended to keep people in his life rather compartmentalized.

JASON. It's kind of a gay thing, don't you think?

SCOTT. *(Involuntarily.)* Yeah. Friends, anyway. —

MICHAEL. *("Graciously.")* Well, now, Rick ... what do you do when you're not *nursing*?

RICK. I'm an art student. Part time. Larry encouraged me to enroll in Parsons. He said if I'd go he'd pay for my tuition.

MICHAEL. I see. — *(HANK reacts with mild surprise. BERNARD looks to HANK. MICHAEL looks to SCOTT again — who turns away again — then to DONALD. Remembers; generally.)* Oh, uh, there are some hot hors d'oeuvres! — I don't know where my mind is.

DONALD. *(Re: SCOTT.) I* do.

*(MICHAEL shoots DONALD a look.)*

EMORY. *(To RICK; French pronunciation for "design.")* Michael has Cuisine "Duhzine" do the food! I love their takeout! They make the best Vol-Au-Vent. *(RICK stares at him blankly. NOTE: the name of the caterer is "Cuisine Design," but pronounced, as if in French. Getting up, sighs.)* Well, if no one else is going to do it.... So what else is nouvelle?

MICHAEL. *Don't* use the microwave.

EMORY. *(Very American accent.)* Jamais, sheree. It dries 'em out.

*(EMORY exits to the kitchen.)*

BERNARD. *(To MICHAEL.)* Is Larry's mother coming?

MICHAEL. *(Shakes his head.)* Had to get back to Philadelphia.

HANK. — The older brother never liked me. He "disapproved." I called him when Larry got sick, but it was the same old story. I'm not surprised he didn't show. But Larry's mother and stepfather managed to get here before he died. They stayed with us ... I mean, with me. — *(BERNARD comes over to HANK, puts his arm around him and comforts him. The group watches stoically. Quietly appreciative.)* Thanks, Bernard. This may sound strange, but you know, even after all these years I can't say I really knew Larry all that well. Do you find that some sort of demented statement?

BERNARD. No.

SCOTT. *(To no one in particular.)* Who ever knows anybody? You never know what's really going on with someone.

HANK. *(Absently.)* Yeah. —

*(MICHAEL takes note of SCOTT's remark.)*

BERNARD. I think we always keep some part of ourselves *to* ourselves.

HANK. — Larry had his secrets, of course. But that, in its way, had its allure. He was always a little bit of a mystery to me. And, I think, to a degree, to himself too.

BERNARD. I sure don't think I know myself. —

JASON. Does anyone, really?

BERNARD. — I mean ... I don't think I can *explain* myself.

HANK. I know that even at my age I'm still finding out things about myself.

RICK. Me, too.

HANK. Now that it's over, I feel relief. And that's the truth. I feel so *relieved* that the nightmare is finally fucking over.

*(A moment of silence. EMORY enters with a silver tray of canapés. All heads swivel to him—a repeat of the opening tableau when he*

*coughed. The room is hushed. All heads follow EMORY as he crosses to HANK.)*

EMORY. *(To HANK.)* Doughnut, soldier? — Sorry, *finger food?*
HANK. *(Has to laugh.)* No, thanks, Emory.

*(EMORY passes among the group.)*

EMORY. — Cheese puffs? Meatballs? Rumaki? — If that dates me, how about: cellulars, nicotine patches, sex toys?
RICK. *(Re: the tray of food.)* Very artistic, Emory. — The presentation.
EMORY. I'm a born stylist.

*(There are reactions of "Mmmm." Some take a canapé and a paper napkin from him, some do not. He comes to MICHAEL, who does not take anything, just stares icily at him ....)*

MICHAEL. You used the microwave, didn't you?
EMORY. No, I didn't.
MICHAEL. *Liar.*
HANK. *(Picking up thought.)* — The time had long since past when we were physical with each other, but emotionally, we couldn't have been closer. He wanted to die. And he wanted me to *help* him die.
RICK. *(To HANK.)* And did you?
HANK. I would never to able to go on living with myself if I'd actually fed him the pills. — That's funny, because I think I'm capable of *anything* — even killing someone. — Anyway, I agreed to be with him — stay with him up to the point where he would swallow them — but I told him I wanted to leave before he did.
JASON. You have to be so careful of the fucking law.
HANK. — I said I'd give him a scrambled egg so there'd be a little something in his stomach — give him a Dramamine so that he

wouldn't vomit and strangle. But he'd have to actually *do* it himself. Swallow the pills alone. But in the end he didn't.

MICHAEL. *(Looks at his watch.)* Oh, where the hell is Harold?!

JASON. He must be caught in the rain.

EMORY. Oh, rain or shine, Harold'll be late for his *own* memorial.

BERNARD. I saw him at the service. — Didn't you see him, Donald?

DONALD. *(Nods.)* With something very blond. — Well, from the neck up.

*(The front door buzzer sounds....)*

MICHAEL. Speak of the devil.

*(MICHAEL goes to the panel beside the front door down right, presses a release button, tears open the door and goes out into the hallway.)*

HANK. *(To no one in particular.)* — Larry conned every doctor in town out of pills. He made sure he had a stash. He never told anybody, and he never took them. Not a single one. — But he made sure he had them ... and yet, he wouldn't take them. — Explain that.

EMORY. I'd have had Kevorkian on the speed dial.

*(MICHAEL returns.)*

EMORY. Is it Hallie?

MICHAEL. No, it's the super. — Scott, did you chain your bike in the entry?

SCOTT. Yeah, to the radiator. Why, is it in the way?

MICHAEL. He wants to mop up the rainwater or something. Bring it up here.

*(SCOTT puts his glass on the stair rung, crosses and goes out.*

*MICHAEL shuts the door.)*

HANK. *(Weeps.)* — Forgive me, I seem to be the only one wallowing in this.
DONALD. Don't be ridiculous, Hank.

*(BERNARD helps sit HANK down, takes HANK's handkerchief out of his jacket pockets and dries his eyes for him.)*

HANK. *(Re: his tears.)* I'm sorry, I really am. This is supposed to be a "Celebration of Life."
EMORY. Frankly, if I never attend another "Celebration of Life" as long as I live, it'll be too fucking soon! — And *if* I receive another invitation to a "Celebration of Life," I *hope* there's a scratch-and-sniff cyanide capsule enclosed! — These post-funeral "Cocktail Huddles" only make you wonder who's next?!
BERNARD. How can you say such a thing!
EMORY. I'm just saying for *me*, all these things have begun to blur. — I know it sounds polit ...
MICHAEL. If you say "politically incorrect," I'm going to rip out your tongue and slice it for sandwiches.

*(The sound of a key in the lock in the front door is heard. The door is opened by SCOTT, who rolls his bike inside and recloses it. He leans it against the wall. JASON crosses to the bike, stoops to "investigate" it.)*

JASON. *(Re: SCOTT's bike.)* There's not a mark on it. Looks just like it did the night I sold it to you. From the way you were talking, I thought ....
SCOTT. It's just the idea that it was stolen out of my apartment that made me feel so ....
JASON. It had to be an inside job. — Maybe one of your friends was just playing a trick on you. After all, it was returned to you.

SCOTT. I found it in the foyer of my building. Lying under the stairs, like it'd been dumped.

*(SCOTT looks to see MICHAEL is staring at him and JASON. So is RICK. SCOTT moves away from JASON and remains apart from the group as EMORY bites loudly into a celery stalk. Everyone turns to stare at him.)*

HANK. *(Continuing.)* — Larry loved his students and by God, he would go to class when he really didn't have the strength to even stand up. He taught when he was in such pain most of us would have ...

DONALD. Begged for a morphine drip ....

BERNARD. But Larry was clean and sober. Like Michael and me. We all wound up in different "rooms."

MICHAEL. *(Almost to himself.)* Ah, those rooms. Some dead, some dying.

BERNARD. *(Upbeat.)* But some saved.

HANK. *(Smiles to himself.)* — My son said we needed God in the bullpen, but He was out of town with another team.

MICHAEL. What I don't understand about Christian Science is that you can have a million facelifts, but you won't go to a doctor.

BERNARD. Larry never had a facelift! Some people just look that good.

HANK. And he wasn't a Christian Scientist. He was a Scientologist.

DONALD. He *was*.

HANK. Well, for about five minutes.

BERNARD. He liked to try everything. I'm all for that.

EMORY. Remember when he was in EST? — Once upon a time. *(To JASON.)* I know you weren't born yet, so just cut me in half and count the rings.

BERNARD. *(Re: drugs and booze.)* And he *Just Said No* up until he had to be taken to the hospital and then other people — doctors —

started making the decisions.

RICK. *(Reflectively.)* I only met him after he was first hospitalized.

JASON. Did he ever come to terms with it?

BERNARD. Come to terms with what?

JASON. Being ashamed of what he had?

HANK. Ashamed?

JASON. — Come on, guys, we've really got to get over this stigma thing.

*(A slight pause ....)*

BERNARD. Larry didn't die of AIDS.

JASON. Well, I know that's the official story.

BERNARD. That's the *true* story! He died of *cancer*.

MICHAEL. — Cancer without the "quotes." The respectable kind. The *esteemed* kind. The kind you get where it doesn't show.

EMORY. Pancreatic.

RICK. — Yeah, that's what was on his chart.

JASON. I though it was ....

MICHAEL. We know what you thought! Gay men *do* die of other things! They do die of prostate tumors and heart attacks and get blown up on planes and all the rest of those good things, just like real people!

EMORY. Or they're *murdered*.

MICHAEL. Or — they just die of old age. Their medical profiles are impeccable but they're so old that when they pee, sand comes out.

DONALD. *(Absently.)* The thing about a real good heart attack is that it's fast.

EMORY. The good thing about Alzheimer's is that you get to hide your own Easter eggs.

BERNARD. What's good about *that*?

EMORY. Forget it. *(Realizes.)* — Sorry!

HANK. What's good about cancer?

BERNARD. Nothing, except it's possible to beat it, and that's good.

EMORY. *(Generally.)* You can get over a heart attack. Michael did.

JASON. *(Sarcastically.)* You can't get over a *fatal* one. *(To EMORY.)* — Are you sure Michael had a heart attack. Maybe it was just a pain down in his arm from the weight of his Rolex.

MICHAEL. You'll be happy to know I can't afford a Rolex and disappointed to hear I *do* have a heart.

JASON. It's only disappointing that you have such a *strong* one. — You know, Michael, you may be the most cynical person I've ever encountered....

MICHAEL. Then they oughtta let you out more often!

BERNARD. *Please.* Could we just ....

MICHAEL. — I see no reason for *"Forced Family Fun."* Must we *pretend* to be gay — and by that I mean it in the linguistically traditional sense of the word, gay?!

JASON. That is the one thing you'll never have to pretend, in any sense.

EMORY. *(Privately amused, to JASON, coyly.)* Oh, you're *terrible*! — But I like you.

JASON. *(Heated.)* I'm sick of self-centered retros like you, who wouldn't get their Guccis stepped on, fighting for what they believe that are ...

HANK. *(Rises, the peacemaker.)* Now, wait a minute, fellas! This is not why we're here. —

MICHAEL. I'm beginning to wonder why some of us *are* here.

RICK. You mean me.

MICHAEL. *(Bluntly, tolerantly.)* I *said* you were welcome!

JASON. He means *me*. He's never liked me and never liked the fact that Larry liked me.

MICHAEL. *(Testily.)* Doesn't anyone of this enlightened generation know how rude it is to refer to someone in the third person who happens to be standing in his presence.

THE MEN FROM THE BOYS 25

JASON. You hate me and my political agenda. And you hated my relationship with Larry — which was none of your goddamn business.
MICHAEL. You didn't even know what he died of! What *relationship*?!
JASON. We were friends. Sometimes *loving* friends. At one time Larry and I happened to be what he called "occasional regulars."

*(HANK looks away.)*

RICK. Does that mean what I think it means?
JASON. It means what it means. I mostly bumped into him at Fire Island. —
EMORY. Are people still going there?
JASON. You can't kill human nature. You can *die* of it, but you can't kill it.
EMORY. *(Placating JASON.)* I see nothing wrong with patrolling the lush, dark, tedious Pines — if you play safe....
BERNARD. *(To EMORY, bluntly.)* You have hookers. That's hardly safe!
EMORY. I do not!
BERNARD. Bullshit. You don't know whether they're going to infect you or cut your fucking throat.
JASON. — When I saw him in the hospital, I was blown away. He'd been so hot ... for an older guy. *(To MICHAEL.)* — So I made a mistake about what he died of! So, sue me!
MICHAEL. It's the city *you* ought to sue — for those legs.
JASON. What?
MICHAEL. You've got Sue-The-City-Legs. You ought to sue the city for building the sidewalk so close to your ass!
DONALD. *(To MICHAEL.)* You ought to keep your personality on a leash.
MICHAEL. You thought he'd been punished by God for his way of life!

JASON. That sounds more like something *you'd* think. I'm just sorry I jumped to a conclusion.

EMORY. If you're going to jump, you may as well dive. — It gives a better line.

JASON. *(To HANK.)* I went to Larry's funeral *because* of the feeling I had for him. *(To MICHAEL.)* And I'm *here* because of it. Throw me out if you want to! *You're* not my friend! Larry was! I'm here for *him*. — And for myself.

BERNARD. If this is going to turn into something other than what it's meant to be, I'm going home. I've learned my lesson in this living room.

MICHAEL. Yeah, here we are back in the same old living room.

BERNARD. *(Moving to leave.)* With the same old queens!

DONALD. Wait, Bernard ... we're *all* upset.

EMORY. And you're all acting like kids!

HANK. *(After a moment.)* — Well, the grown-ups are acting like kids. The kids are acting quite grown-up. Rick has barely opened his mouth. And Scott hasn't said a word at all. — *(SCOTT shifts uncomfortably, crosses to the bar cart to pick up a Diet Coke and go behind the stairs, his back to the group. Calmly.)* Look ... we're here to share our sorrow and we're free to act as angry and frustrated and scared and sad and depressed as we feel.

MICHAEL. *(Musically, "great star" largesse; lovely smile.)* — And as "happy." — *(For JASON's benefit.)* Or ... we're free to feel just as sad as if he *had* died of AIDS.

DONALD. *(To MICHAEL.)* Why don't you have a double Shirley Temple and cool it.

*(MICHAEL bristles at DONALD's remark. The door buzzes.)*

EMORY. Well, final*ment*!

*(EMORY sits on the floor, behind the coffee table, leaning against the sofa. MICHAEL goes to press the release button, opens the front*

*door, goes out into the hallway.)*

HANK. Is it Harold?
MICHAEL. *(Offstage.)* No. Flowers, I think.
JASON. Who needs a refill?

*(JASON goes to the bar cart, takes the Dom Perignon out of its cooler and goes to refill glasses — HANK's, EMORY's, RICK's. MICHAEL returns with beautiful, elegantly arranged, home-grown cut flowers in a vase.)*

EMORY. *(Impressed.)* Oh, my, who sent that?!
MICHAEL. Do I know? They're for Hank.
EMORY. I can live without food, but I can't live without flowers.
BERNARD. Then you better lay off the chocolate-covered nasturtiums.

*(HANK opens the card.)*

HANK. *(Reads card.)* They're from Patsy and Jessica.
EMORY. The butch dykes who run the animal clinic? *(Quickly corrects.)* — The rather male-identified professional women in the country …?
RICK. *(To MICHAEL re: flowers.)* Where're you going to put them.
EMORY. Well, Lady Astor always said, "Build a garden under a lamp." *And she oughtta know.*

*(MICHAEL gives EMORY a look, plonks the bouquet in the middle of the coffee table, completely covering EMORY from view.)*

JASON. *(To EMORY.)* Don't you have any consciousness at all?
EMORY. *(Rising into view.)* I'm kidding, for Christ's sake!! That was a joke, you serious, solemn, sex machine! — *Although*, I must tell you, dykes do not eat egg salad sandwiches and they don't pack their

clothes in tissue paper. *That* is a verite.

*(BERNARD looks away. JASON shakes his head.)*

HANK. *(Ignoring everyone.)* — I haven't been to the country for weeks, and Patsy and Jessica have been so good about the dogs and the plants and the pipes — they've really taken care of the place for us. — Well, for me, now.

JASON. I don't know that gay men are going to be as supportive. Can you see us marching for breast cancer?

DONALD. Yeah, we're not really interested in their culture — I mean, we don't read lesbian novels or see the latest lesbian film, when it's almost a supposition that they support gay men's art. —

MICHAEL. Gay guys are so much more self-involved. They'll just continue in their me-me-me, gym-gym-gym, sex-sex-sex, business-as-usual way.

HANK. *(Continuing.)* — Larry was only sixty. That's too young to die.

RICK. With all due respect, that's old to me. He seemed so much younger.

JASON. *(To HANK.)* Was he really sixty?

HANK. He knocked a few years off, but he was sixty. It was hard for him to get old. He was the kind of guy who was meant to be young and handsome forever.

MICHAEL. There's no such thing as fair — there's just luck. If I had to be born at all, I'd rather been born male than female, rich rather that poor, straight instead of gay. It would have made life much easier *not* to have been gay. *(Looks at BERNARD.)* — And some of us got a double whammy, right Bernard?

BERNARD. I'm surprised you didn't say, "Some of us got it in spades." If you want to hate, there's always something to hate about everybody.

MICHAEL. — I'd rather be white instead of black, brown, yellow or red. And that's just the way I feel. — I'd rather be gentile rather than Jewish, Protestant rather than Catholic. Actually I'd rather have been religion-free.... *(RICK, DONALD react.)* — It's *easier* that way.

DONALD. What's so great about the easy way out?

MICHAEL. Only a fool would want the *hard* way out. — I'd rather be good-looking instead of plain — why couldn't we all truly have been created equal? It would have been just as easy, but, oh, no, that's not life. Some of us had to be born "interesting." And some of us, *not* so interesting. Some of us flat-out ugly. Some of us started out okay and wound up like toads. I want it easy! I want it all aces. I want something not so uphill as ... life, *grinding, luckless life!*

JASON. You need help, Michael. Professional help. Your mind is like a bad neighborhood. You shouldn't go in there alone.

EMORY. *(To JASON, re: MICHAEL.)* He's here, he's veneer, get used to it.

*(RICK crosses to the terrace doors, looks out....)*

RICK. It's stopped raining. —
DONALD. Yeah, why don't we all move outside?
SCOTT. Good idea, it's getting pretty stale in here.
DONALD. Michael has sucked all they oxygen out of the air. That's about all he's permitted to do these days.

*(MICHAEL ignores DONALD as JASON opens the doors.)*

MICHAEL. Emory just blew a fucking fortune fluffing it up up for the summer.

EMORY. *(Gets up.)* I want to see if that hunky guy from the nursery did just what I told him to do with the pots of geraniums.

JASON. I'd kill for a cigarette.

BERNARD. Me, too, but my wife and I finally gave it up. Booze first, then tobacco.

JASON. Your wife?

HANK. *(Offhandedly.)* Things change.

BERNARD. — She was my first sponsor.

JASON. You met her in a twelve-step program?

BERNARD. *(Nods.)* It was a slow process. We'd both been hurt — and dealt with it the wrong way. So ... we talked a long time, and then lived together a long time, and then.... I'm sorry she couldn't be here. She's in Detroit with my mother, who's not well.

JASON. *(Curiously.)* She know you're ... well, whatever it is you are?

BERNARD. *(Smile, nods.)* We know all about each other. She was married to a very nice, ordinary guy, but she says he treated her in a way that was ... well, like what you might call "sexual bigotry" — although he didn't have a clue. He just behaved that way as a matter of course. With me, she says she feels like an equal. We have fun together. *(With meaning.)* All kinds of fun. —

JASON. Are you happy?

BERNARD. *(Drolly.)* You mean, in spite of my flying in the face of being gay and "going hetero"?

JASON. I'm just trying to understand.

BERNARD. Well, then ... I guess I've come to think happiness is habit. And so, yeah. — And, yeah, we love each other but, more important, we're each other's best friend. — I use to not like sleeping with my friends — the people I laughed with and told everything to. But now, she's the only person I actually trust. And, oh, yeah, "the other" sometimes goes through my mind, but I've been there. And it didn't work out. I guess something could happen again, but I'm not planning on it.

EMORY. *(Quietly.)* But, *I'm* your best friend.

BERNARD. *(Calmly, sincerely.)* No, I'm *your* best friend. You're my best *male* friend. *(To JASON.)* — I have to admit — it all scares the shit out of me.

EMORY. *(Sighs.)* Yeah. Like finding your own shade of rouge.

*(JASON removes a pack of cigarettes and goes outside.)*

## THE MEN FROM THE BOYS 31

RICK. I could stay in this room forever. — This must be what they call "soignee."
BERNARD. I think this child has been seduced by décor.
EMORY. *(With meaning.)* It wouldn't be the first time.

*(BERNARD gives EMORY a look as EMORY exits to terrace. RICK wanders the room, studying things. The phone rings.)*

MICHAEL. *(Into phone.)* Hello? — Yeah ... oh, *hi*! — Yeah, he's fine.
HANK. I bet that's my son. —

*(RICK stops, looks up.)*

MICHAEL. *(Into phone.)* We'll see that he gets home. —— You both looked great too. Sorry you can't drop by, but I understand. Let me know when the big day arrives. Promise? Right. — Bye. *(Hangs up. To HANK.)* It's too uncomfortable for Kate to get around till the baby comes.
DONALD. When's it due?
HANK. Any minute.
BERNARD. Hank's second grandchild!

*(BERNARD crosses to check on HANK as RICK watches, curiously. JASON takes out a cigarette, puts it between his lips, exits to the terrace, searching his pockets for matches. HANK drops his head and turns away.)*

EMORY. *(Loudly, off stage.)* — That goddamn dumb, musclebound, son-of-a-bitch from the nursery!! I told him no fucking vulgar Puerto Rican pink geraniums!! I said I only wanted pale Martha Washington colors!! — But what did *he* know about *subtlety*!!

*(HANK dries his eyes, hands the handkerchief to BERNARD....)*

HANK. *(Re: handkerchief.)* Thanks, Bernard.
BERNARD. That's yours, baby.

*(BERNARD takes the handkerchief and tucks it in HANK's suit breast pocket.)*

HANK. *(Nods.)* Oh, yeah, so it is. Thanks.
EMORY. *(Enters, almost in tears.)* This Celebration of Life is ruined! Just *ruined*!

*(EMORY whips back outside. HANK looks to see RICK staring at him. They exchange a smile.)*

DONALD. *(To RICK, flirting.)* I thought you wanted some air.
RICK. *(Forces a smile.)* I do. How about you?
DONALD. *(With a twinkle.)* Yeah, I'd love to come up for air.

*(MICHAEL takes stock of DONALD as he goes outside, buzzing in RICK's ear.)*

EMORY. *(Offstage, outraged.)* I ... DON'T ... FUCKING ... *BELIEVE IT*!!!

*(MICHAEL has crossed to the stairs and SCOTT.)*

MICHAEL. Champagne?
SCOTT. No, thank you.
MICHAEL. Not even for your birthday?
SCOTT. My birthday was two weeks ago.
MICHAEL. I know very well when your birthday was. Since we haven't spoken, I was wondering how it went.
SCOTT. As you might expect, thanks to my father.
MICHAEL. And how *is* your father?
SCOTT. The same. After he asked me what I wanted for my

birthday and I told him, he didn't give me anything.
MICHAEL. He didn't give you a present of *any* kind?
SCOTT. He blustered into my place drunk; didn't even shake my hand.
MICHAEL. It seems that all you can really count on with him is for him to let you down. *(He puts his hand on SCOTT's shoulder as DONALD enters from the terrace. SCOTT sees DONALD, shrugs off MICHAEL's hand. MICHAEL looks at DONALD. To DONALD, re: RICK.)* How are you, shall we say, making out?
DONALD. *(Re: SCOTT's shrug.)* I'd say about the same as you. — The chairs are all wet.
MICHAEL. *(With an edge.)* I'd say get some towels and dry them off.
DONALD. Right. *(Finishes his drink.)* First things first.

*(DONALD goes to the bar cart and freshens his martini for MICHAEL's benefit. MICHAEL makes a disapproving face as EMORY flies inside.)*

EMORY. *(Petulantly.)* — What are we having to eat? I'm absolutely rav!
MICHAEL. Just some chicken hash and a little endive and watercress salad.

*(RICK re-enters.)*

EMORY. *(Flirty, to RICK.)* Richarr, shall you and I heat up the Cuisine "Duhzine"?
RICK. Why don't I just wipe off the chairs. I'm better at cleaning up.

*(Crestfallen, EMORY exits to the kitchen. DONALD crosses to stairs, drink in hand.)*

DONALD. *(To MICHAEL, with disgusted awe.)* — Caterers and decorators.
MICHAEL. *(Defensively.)* I just got a job!
DONALD. And you're already spending what you haven't made yet.
MICHAEL. *(Dismissive.)* Yeah-yeah-yeah.
DONALD. I thought you told me you had to dip into your pension fund because you hadn't work in so long.
MICHAEL. I did. Anyone who doesn't live beyond his means suffers from a lack of imagination!

*(DONALD gives SCOTT a look, goes upstairs and into the bath.)*

SCOTT. *(Re: DONALD.)* He's jealous of me, isn't he?
MICHAEL. He's jealous of *me*. He just resents *you*.
SCOTT. Well, he doesn't have to feel threatened by *me*.

*(MICHAEL is silent. SCOTT finishes his Diet Coke. MICHAEL turns to the group.)*

MICHAEL. *(Graciously, but swallowing dryly.)* How're everybody's drinks?
HANK. *(Holds up empty flute.)* Mind if I get a beer?
MICHAEL. Of course not. There's some in the fridge. *(HANK exits to the kitchen. Sotto, to SCOTT.)* — I was genuinely happy that you called this morning and suggested we go to the service together. I wanted to see you before I left for California.
SCOTT. Is it a good job?
MICHAEL. Just a TV rewrite.
SCOTT. How long will you be gone?
MICHAEL. A month or so.
SCOTT. *(After a moment.)* — I'm so confused about our so-called friendship. —
MICHAEL. Scott, I really don't think this is the proper time to

get into all that.
SCOTT. Do I have to make an appointment?

*(BERNARD and RICK look up. MICHAEL turns to them, smiles awkwardly. BERNARD takes a soft drink, opens it. MICHAEL turns away.)*

MICHAEL. No. — You don't have to make an appointment. *(After a moment.)* Why don't you go up to the bedroom, and I'll come up in a minute.
SCOTT. I think I'd just better leave.
MICHAEL. No, Scott, please, don't.
SCOTT. *(After a moment.)* I'm sorry I forgot to put the ice out.

*(DONALD comes downstairs to hear MICHAEL's plea. They exchange an uneasy look.)*

DONALD. *(Hands over towels.)* Here, Rick, start on the chairs, I'll get the cushions.

*(RICK exits to the terrace with the towels.)*

MICHAEL. *(Sotto, to SCOTT.)* — Please? — Go on. I'll be up in a minute.

*(SCOTT crushes his Diet Coke can, passes DONALD on the stairs, goes up, tearing off his T-shirt, continuing off into the bathroom. The bedroom light fades.)*
DONALD. *(Re: SCOTT.)* It'll never work.
MICHAEL. Why?
DONALD. Because he doesn't make you laugh.
MICHAEL. *(Shaken, edgy.)* Something you read in a book? — Or has the booze finally reached what's left of your wet brain?

*(MICHAEL glares at DONALD, as EMORY exits the kitchen with a stack of ceramic plates.)*

EMORY. *(Sing-song.)* Behind you!

*(MICHAEL moves aside to let EMORY pass as JASON enters from the terrace, exhaling from a discarded cigarette. He waves his hand to disperse the smoke.)*

JASON. It's nice out.
EMORY. *(Whizzing past.)* Then *leave* it out!

*(EMORY exits to the terrace. In the bedroom SCOTT paces, sits on the bed, the quickly gets up, smoothes the cover. Downstairs, DONALD replenishes his drink.)*

MICHAEL. *(Not to DONALD.)* — Will somebody roll the bar outside and get the wine while I see about the food?
JASON. If you'll cease fire, I'll do the bar. — I'm good at it, remember?
MICHAEL. *(Lightly, but unrelenting.)* You're sure you don't have a date on a float somewhere? — *(Sighs, to JASON.)* Okay ... time out. *(Indicates up right wall.)* The corkscrew and wine buckets are in the cabinet. — The wine's in the fridge.

*(JASON goes up right to an "invisible" cabinet: doors seamlessly cut into the photo blowup wall. He throws them open to reveal glass shelves which light-up and contain a stupefying supply of liquor and glasses.)*

BERNARD. *(Reacts with anxious dismay.)* Good Christ, Michael!

*(MICHAEL remains completely cool.)*

MICHAEL. *(Sardonically.)* A fully stocked bar is a happy bar. — Besides, these days, you never know when there's going to be another Celebration of Life!

*(HANK enters from the kitchen with a bottle of beer in hand....)*

BERNARD. *(Unnerved, re: bar.)* The sight of that is *staggering* — in the classic sense of the word!
MICHAEL. *(Facetiously.)* A sip is not a slip. Is it, Bernard?
BERNARD. *(angrily.) You're not serious!!*
MICHAEL. *(Surprised and touched, actually.)* Oh, Bernard, I'm *kidding*! — Did I upset you?
DONALD. Of course you upset him!
MICHAEL. Well, I didn't mean to. It's just my warped sense of humor.
BERNARD. You're playing with fucking dynamite, man! How much time do you have?
MICHAEL. Seven years.
BERNARD. I slipped at nine!
MICHAEL. Oh, Bernard, I don't want to drink or use! But there's something comforting about having liquor on the premises. Like having prescription drugs. You just know they're there. I'd panic if there weren't any anesthetics in the house.
BERNARD. You sound like Harold.
HANK. Or Larry.
BERNARD. *(Quietly controlled.)* Fucking dynamite, man! Everything you say or do!
MICHAEL. I know and I'm sorry, okay?! I apologize!
BERNARD. *(Levelly.)* It's all right to hate, Michael. It's just not all right to act in a hateful way.

*(BERNARD exits to the terrace, fuming.)*

MICHAEL. *(Re: BERNARD's reaction.)* Christ of the Andes!

Where did *that* come from?

DONALD. *It wasn't funny.*

MICHAEL. What about *you*. Still knocking them back as if time had stood still! *(Re: BERNARD.)* Why doesn't he say something to *you*!

DONALD. I *want* to drink, Michael.

MICHAEL. Well, so do I, but I can't because I'm a drunk!

DONALD. And so am *I* and so *what*?! *(Drains his glass.)* Bernard understands this conversation is out-of-bounds. Larry would have — why can't you?!

*(MICHAEL restrains himself. JASON, having found the corkscrew and wine bucket, exits to kitchen. DONALD goes up right center to another "invisible door," opens it and removes some new, smartly upholstered exterior chair cushions.)*

BERNARD. *(Offstage.)* — Hey, Rick, my man, you really *do* know how to mop up!

RICK. *(Offstage.)* Well, I've cleaned enough toilets in my time.

BERNARD. *(Offstage.)* Yeah, what's one more or less, huh.

*(MICHAEL stiffens, exchanges a look with DONALD, who closes the cabinet doors and exits to the terrace with the seat cushions.*
*HANK has gone to the étagère and put on a CD of Ella Fitzgerald's "Skylark"\* or similar style recording, which starts to play. JASON enters with several bottles of white wine which he puts on the bar cart, starts to roll it outside. EMORY enters from the terrace as JASON starts to lift the bar cart over the threshold....)*

EMORY. *(To JASON.)* Need a hand, big boy?

JASON. Thanks.

EMORY. I take it that you work out.

---

\*References to recordings or songs in this acting edition do not constitute permission to use the song(s) in your production. Synchronization rights for use of any music within the production must be obtained from the copyright holder.

## THE MEN FROM THE BOYS

JASON. Yeah, American Fitness.
EMORY. *(Nods, knowingly, play-on-words.) Or*, as we say: "Oh-Mary-Can-Ya-Lift-This" — ? The fit American goes to American Fitness. That's why Eighth Avenue between Fourteenth and Twenty-third looks like an open call for *Spartacus, the Musical.*

*(They lift the bar cart over the jamb and exit to the terrace. MICHAEL sees HANK has picked up a photograph in a silver frame on the étagère and is looking at it. MICHAEL comes over to HANK....)*

HANK. *(Re: Scott's photo.)* He's a handsome kid, Michael.
MICHAEL. — Scott's aunt took that of us.
HANK. He introduced you to his family?
MICHAEL. He just wanted me to meet his aunt. She's all he cares about — the only one who's ever been the least bit kind to him. We took her to lunch. I loaned Scott my dark blue cashmere blazer, and he looked so elegant. — His aunt was so proud of him. She held his hand on the top of the table for a long time after the plates had been cleared away, and he didn't seem uncomfortable at all.
HANK. Is he uncomfortable at a show of affection?
MICHAEL. From some people. At a genuine show of affection, I guess. *(Sardonically.)* I wouldn't know a thing about that.
HANK. He looks *very* proud of you, Michael.

*(MICHAEL smiles, takes the picture of Scott from HANK, turns and goes up the stairs.*
*HANK now picks up a photograph of Larry and studies it a moment. DONALD and RICK come inside. RICK watches HANK.)*

DONALD. *(To HANK.)* Nice shot of Larry.
HANK. I think so. Brazil was great. We had a good time there.

*(HANK replaces the photograph and exits to the terrace. RICK goes*

*to the étagère, picks up the framed photograph of Larry. — Suddenly, RICK dissolves into tears. DONALD goes to him, puts his arm around him.)*

RICK. *(Distraught.)* Oh, God, Donald, what am I going to do?!
DONALD. What you *can't* do is let Hank see you break down.
RICK. *(Sobbing.)* I loved him.
DONALD. I know you did. — Sort of like the hostage/captor syndrome in reverse, I guess.
RICK. Please, don't joke! — I helped him die. He begged me to turn up the drip till he was gone — then turn it down before I called the doctor. I *couldn't*. I ... I ... put some morphine suppositories on this bedside table, then I left the room. — When I came back, I took the empty foil wrappers and flushed them down the toilet so no one would know. Then, I did what he told me. I called the doctor. *(RICK falls against DONALD, sobs. DONALD puts his arms about RICK, kisses him on his cheek, forehead and, finally, sweetly on the mouth. RICK responds passionately. — JASON enters with the empty ice bucket, stops on a dime, watches them. — RICK's head goes limp on DONALD's shoulder.)* I wonder who else knows I loved him?
DONALD. I don't think anyone *here* knows ... *(Looks up at JASON.)* — Well ....
JASON. I don't know a thing. Not a thing.
RICK. *(Recovering.)* There's nothing to know, really, except that I ... felt about Larry the way I do. I think he just liked the idea that I was crazy about him. — *(To DONALD.)* — You never told Michael, did you?
DONALD. *Of course not.*

*(JASON turns and exits to the kitchen.)*

RICK. *(Looks at photo of Larry.)* He was so much fun. When he was in remission, after his classes, we had kind of a standing date. Nothing much, really — Starbuck's, the movies, my place. — He was

so loving. *(Through tears.)* But I knew it could never lead to anything. *(He puts the photo back on the shelf.)* — Hank never knew. He hardly remembers me. — I'm sorry about this ... acting like this....
DONALD. I understand.
RICK. Thanks, Donald. I hope you don't get the wrong idea.
DONALD. What's a little kiss between friends?

*(They get a grip. JASON enters, the ice bucket refilled.)*

RICK. Have you seen my guitar case?
JASON. *(Nods.)* In the kitchen. You gonna sing us that song?
RICK. I'm gonna sing somebody that song.

*(RICK goes in the kitchen.)*

JASON. — So, Bernard says you live in the Hamptons. I'm house sitting for a friend out there.
DONALD. Well, you ought to give me a call. We could have a picnic on the beach ....
JASON. It's still a little chilly for that, isn't it?
DONALD. I could make a thermos of martinis.
JASON. I'm in the program.
DONALD. Not you too! You're like the pod people!
JASON. *(Laughs.)* There's only Michael and Bernard and me left. Three out of nine — that's not such a frightening average. And *I'm* a bartender!
DONALD. Keep up the good work!
JASON. I feel like such an enabler. — You know, what's wrong with this picture?!
DONALD. — I'll give you my phone number anyway. —

*(DONALD and JASON go outside onto the terrace in conversation. Lights begin to fad as RICK exits the kitchen with his guitar. He strums a few chords, goes onto the terrace.*

*Lights fade out downstairs, come up in the bedroom as SCOTT exits the bathroom, pulling on one of MICHAEL's expensive cashmere sweaters. He sees MICHAEL put down the photograph of them.)*

SCOTT. — My T-shirt was damp. Mind if I borrow this? *(MICHAEL shakes his head.)* — You cleaned out the medicine cabinet. —

MICHAEL. *I* didn't. Maybe the maid did. — Looking for something?

SCOTT. I kinda got a headache. — *(After an awkward pause....)* — Listen, I quit school.

MICHAEL. I know. I was wondering if you were going to tell me.

SCOTT. How do you know? Did one of those old bastards ...?

MICHAEL. No, I went to meet you after class last week. I thought we ought to have a chat and clear the air. You weren't there.

SCOTT. N.Y.U. was a mistake. I was in over my head. I couldn't cut it.

MICHAEL. It's my fault for insisting.

SCOTT. No, it's not. I like it that you cared. It's more than my own father did. I think I need to work outdoors. Landscape gardening. Or maybe I could be a vet. Maybe you could introduce me to those friends of Hank's in the Hamptons.

MICHAEL. Sure. — *Anything.* But, Scott, *study something.* You've got a good mind.

SCOTT. — Listen, I think I'm going to slip out now. You know, parties — well, whatever you call this — are just not my thing. *(MICHAEL nods.)* — Now I suppose you're going to drop the bomb.

MICHAEL. *(After a moment.)* I'm simply going to try to tell you how I feel. — Unless there is some physical contact, some show of ... *affection* ... between us ... I can't ....

SCOTT. — Here it comes.

MICHAEL. What does "drop the bomb" really mean?

SCOTT. What do you think?

MICHAEL. Well ... I think you think that it means you will be emotionally betrayed. *Abandoned* — which seems to be the major theme of your life.

SCOTT. Michael, just say what's on your mind and I'll go.

MICHAEL. I've said it.

SCOTT. *(Sheepishly.)* You want me to go now?

MICHAEL. *(Sharply.)* Scott, *make sense*! You knew from the start how I felt about you!

SCOTT. Knew what *you* wanted, you mean!

MICHAEL. Yes! I've never tried to hide what I wanted. And in spite of the "threat" to you, you allowed things to progress.

SCOTT. Threat?

MICHAEL. *(Impatiently.)* You heard me. *Threat.* A show of those feeling from me, a negative response from you, and my reaction — which to you meant that I would go away and leave you.

*(SCOTT goes to sit on the bed, but the moment he does he gets up and moves to the chair.)*

SCOTT. I don't want any emotional involvement with anyone! Or physical, either! I like you as a friend. Why can't we leave it at that?

MICHAEL. Scott, I don't want to continue in what is a painful and unhappy situation for me. But you don't want to hear that. Because you want all the advantages and none of the responsibilities. — In short, you want me to be a checkbook and an ear. Well, what's in this for *me*!

*(SCOTT gets up, picks up the picture, looks at it.)*

SCOTT. I don't want things to change. In any way. I've told you that my aversion to being touched is not just with you, it's with everybody.

MICHAEL. That's not good enough! — Scott, we were like

lovers without the sex.

SCOTT. My body is my own.

MICHAEL. *(Coolly.)* Well, yes. It is. Yours to keep or to give to whomever you what. And if you don't want to give yourself to me, you must try to understand what that does to me!

SCOTT. Do I have to try in front of all these old farts?!

MICHAEL. I suppose you mean my contemporaries. — And of course, I'm folklore.

SCOTT. I'm sorry. I actually like them. Well, *two* of them. — Well ... *one* of them.

MICHAEL. Chronologically, I am aware that I could be your father. In some climates, possibly your grandfather. —

SCOTT. Age has nothing to do with it. — *Really. (Frustrated.)* — Oh, forget it. — Goodbye. *(SCOTT makes a move toward the stairs, MICHAEL doesn't try to stop him. SCOTT stops, says emphatically ...)* I said, *goodbye.*

MICHAEL. *(As if he's just heard him. Casually.)* — Sorry. Goodbye.

*(SCOTT is silent, sinks to the floor, starts to weep. MICHAEL looks at him for a moment, then goes to lower himself to the floor beside him.)*

SCOTT. It has noting to do with *you*, I've told you that. It's with anybody. *I don't want to be touched*!

MICHAEL. *(Touches SCOTT's knee.)* Are you really that damaged? *(SCOTT recoils.)* — Or am I repulsive to you? Tell me. I can take it. It would be a relief to know what's really going on in your head.

SCOTT. *(Turns away, sobs uncontrollably.)* I can't fight the things that have been done to me.

MICHAEL. Listen, my roots were, I think, uglier than your own — an emotional torment I don't know how I survived.

SCOTT. *(Weeping.)* How'd you do it?

**THE MEN FROM THE BOYS** 45

MICHAEL. I met people who were smarter and wiser than I was, and I learned from them. — Like I've tried to pass on things to you. — *(Directly.)* — Like believing in yourself. — Your *self*: that thing you feel when you go through a revolving door — that post, that center, that something *unshakable* ... around which everything else spins!

*(SCOTT turns to MICHAEL, keeping his distance....)*

SCOTT. *(Through tears.)* I had always hoped ... dreamed that one day I would somehow cross paths with a person like you — someone who'd see something in me. — Don't you think I know you've spent a lot of money on me — all the restaurants and clothes and the classes you've paid for? And don't you know I can't help feeling, in some way, undeserving of all this. *(He starts to dry his eyes, gets to his feet....)* — But I know it'll pay off, though I could never pay you back.

*(MICHAEL stands up next to SCOTT.)*

MICHAEL. *(With meaning.)* Yes, you could.

*(MICHAEL turns back, embraces SCOTT awkwardly. SCOTT is thrown, flustered.)*

SCOTT. *(Jokey, laughs nervously.)* Quick! Fast forward this! —

*(MICHAEL hangs on to him steadfastly....)*

MICHAEL. *(Intense whisper.)* — Be *real*! *(SCOTT violently disentangles himself, stumbles backward awkwardly, flailing his arms, panicked. He almost falls over a chair, almost upsets the bedside table. MICHAEL doesn't move, straightens with a regained dignity. SCOTT recovers, stumbles downstairs, stops in the middle of the room, leans against the sofa, gasping for air. MICHAEL slowly descends the stairs. Looks at SCOTT.)* Breathe! You always stop breathing the moment there's any inference of emotion or sexual demand ....

SCOTT. *(Hyperventilating.)* I can't! —

MICHAEL. Take a breath, goddamit!

SCOTT. *(Gets up, gets his breath.)* I can't help it if I feel like ... like I'm suffocating.

MICHAEL. Well, I wanted many things — but never to asphyxiate you. — I want you to be able to feel something authentic for someone. If not me, then someone else. Even if *you* have to abandon *me*.

SCOTT. *(Not looking at MICHAEL.)* — When I was seventeen, I was already getting into bars with a fake I.D., this guy came on to me — but the more he did, the more I was obnoxious. I don't know when he left the bar, but I stayed till it closed and started walking home. — At a traffic light a car pulled up beside me. It was the guy. He offered me a ride. I know it was stupid, but I got in. He pulled a gun and drove me all the way to his place in Jersey.

MICHAEL. *(Quietly.)* Oh, Christ. —

SCOTT. *(Takes a breath.)* — He ordered me into his house and handcuffed me at gunpoint. He made me take my clothes off, then he shot me up on drugs and loaded a pistol. Then he blindfolded me and fucked me with the barrel. *(Turns to MICHAEL.)* I was so drugged, so scared that it became a sort of "out of body" experience. — When it was over, he uncuffed me and handed me the gun and told me to shoot him for what he'd done.

MICHAEL. Well I certainly hope you *did*.

SCOTT. *(Shakes his head.)*— He tried to make me take money to make up for it. And I refused. Finally, he offered me drugs. And even though I really wanted them, I refused. I pulled on my clothes the best I could and staggered out and just kept trying to put one foot in front of the other. — *(After a moment.)* — Did you know that Emory is working on some very "rah-sha-sha? needlepoint pillow that says,

"Elegance Is Refusal" — ?

MICHAEL. *(Nods sardonically at the "in" joke, re: "recherche.")* Yes, very "rah-sha-sha." *(They both break-up laughing — then, reflectively.)* — I guess, what you told me's enough to make anyone not want to be touched as long as they live.

SCOTT. *(Comes closer to MICHAEL.)* I don't think that's what did it. Of course, that might have sorta topped things off — but I was the way I am before that ever happened. — I'd had sex before then. I just never liked it all that much. — It was never possible for me to combine being physical with someone who I'd let into my confidence. —

MICHAEL. Are you trying to tell me that's why I have the rare privilege of your body *language* rather than your *body*?

SCOTT. *(Comes closer.)* It's the way I am. I'm as queer as I can be and have no problem with that, but I don't like to be touched. I don't like to be stared at. — I won't even shower at the gym after my workout.

MICHAEL. Why, is it too cruisy?

SCOTT. *(Tough.) Life* is cruisy!

MICHAEL. *(After a moment.)* I love you.

SCOTT. *(After a moment.)* And I love you too.

MICHAEL. Well, I guess sometimes, love just isn't enough. *(SCOTT is silent, gets his bicycle, rolls it to the front door....)* You think Jason had a point? You think maybe it was one of your friends who took your bike?

SCOTT. I never have anyone over. You know that. I must have just left my door unlocked by mistake. *(Starts to move, stops....)* — Uh, I hate to ask you this, but can I borrow twenty dollars?

*(MICHAEL takes his wallet out of his pocket without hesitation, gives it to him.)*

MICHAEL. Here — take forty. Or sixty. Take whatever you want.

SCOTT. Forty is enough. *(SCOTT hands the wallet back to MICHAEL. He returns it to his pocket.)* Thanks. — *(Unyielding eye contact.)* I'll never forget what you've gone through with me, and I'm going to try to make sure the effort wasn't for nothing.

MICHAEL. *(Simply.)* Thanks. I care what happens to you.

SCOTT. — I'm sad that I haven't turned out to be what you'd hoped I'd be for you. I'm sad that I still don't know how to love or be loved.

MICHAEL. I hope you find out before you're my age.

*(SCOTT opens the front door, rolls the bike out, and closes the door. MICHAEL doesn't move. HANK has entered to see SCOTT exit, but SCOTT does not see him. MICHAEL turns.)*

HANK. Doesn't Scott want anything to eat before he goes?

MICHAEL. *(After a moment.)* — It's not going to work out, Hank. I think he's gone for good.

HANK. Did he tell you that?

MICHAEL. He didn't have to. He told me that he'd quite school, though. But I already knew. Like I already knew it wasn't going to work out.

HANK. Are you okay?

MICHAEL. Let's see ... what am I? Crushed. Depressed. Suicidal. No, not that. I've always looked for love in inappropriate places. So, yeah, I'm okay. I'm fine. I won't drink over this, if that's what you mean.

HANK. That's what I mean.

MICHAEL. To be honest, I want to but if I did, I might as well put a gun to my head. Not that that wouldn't be a welcome relief. — Anyway, I don't want that. Not *yet*, anyway. So ... not to worry. Hank, I'm that dreaded word ... *survivor*.

HANK. Michael — the love of another person is a discipline not easily won or maintained.

## THE MEN FROM THE BOYS

MICHAEL. But you think it's worth the risk.

HANK. It took a long time for Larry and me to get to that point. — Well that is, it took *me* a long time. But I finally understood what he was driving at. It's so simple. You be you. I'll be me. *But ...* we'll be together.

*(The doorbell rings three times. MICHAEL looks at HANK expectantly, goes to the door and opens it. HAROLD is standing there, not having aged a great deal; still thin, still with kinky black hair. He has on sunglasses, a rain cape and carries a dripping umbrella.)*

MICHAEL. Well, if it isn't the anti-Christ!

HAROLD. I take it you were expecting someone else. I rang thrice so you wouldn't think it was the postman and get all wet and coozy.

MICHAEL. How'd you get in?

HAROLD. Your divine super was mopping up downstairs. Feisty little bugger. I told him I was here for the Yale reunion. He directed me to your apartment.

*(He hands the umbrella to MICHAEL, slips out of his rain cape and hands that to MICHAEL too, as if he were an attendant.)*

BERNARD. *(Enters from terrace.)* What've you been doing with that blond, Harold?

HAROLD. *(Kisses BERNARD.)* Petal!

BERNARD. You're so tanned!

HAROLD. I've been in St. Bart's — playing Dorothy Dandridge in *Island in the Sun.*

MICHAEL. Everybody else came directly from the service! That was an hour ago, at the very least! *(Dumps umbrella and cape.)* There's been time for a deluge! Foyers have been flooded! Arks have been built!

HAROLD. *(Entering.)* Surely you know by now I have absolutely no sense of time.

MICHAEL. If that is true, then why are you never an hour *early*.

BERNARD. Maybe your watch stopped.

HAROLD. *(Looks at his watch.)* I don't think so. It was running perfectly when my man put it on me this morning. — *(Reacting to light.)* — Oh, my *God*, this is real straight-boy lighting. What *is* this, the open-heart surgery room?!

MICHAEL. You're stoned.

*(EMORY pops in from the kitchen with a silver casserole in chafing frame.)*

HAROLD. Hello, d'yah. *(Note: That's "dear" very, very clipped.)*

EMORY. You're just in time for food, Hallie.

HAROLD. Oh-I-can't-eat-a-thing-what-are-you-having?

EMORY. Lean and mean "Cuisine Duhzine."

HAROLD. *(For MICHAEL's benefit.)* Ohh, minced pigs nipples on toast points. From that trendy frog gonif on Second Avenue? *(EMORY hoots, whips outside as DONALD enters. HAROLD passes DONALD en route to HANK. Not looking at DONALD and not stopping.)* — Donald, good to see you.

DONALD. *(With resignation.)* As always, Harold.

*(DONALD goes to the wall bar, removes a stack of Italian ceramic plates. HAROLD comes up to HANK, takes his hands.)*

HAROLD. *(With great feeling.)* Hank. — How are you, bubelah?

HANK. *(Hugs HAROLD.)* Thanks for everything, Harold. I couldn't have arranged it without your help.

HAROLD. What can I tell you, some of my best friends are

morticians. *(Sincerely.)* I wish I could say I know just how you feel. I have no idea how you feel. — That was a terrific little mention in the *Post* on Larry's work.

HANK. I thought so.

EMORY. *(Enters, empty-handed.)* Oh, I didn't see it, and I read the *Post* every day.

HAROLD. It was in the Lifestyle section. We're never news — we're always lifestyles.

*(Outside, RICK begins to strum his guitar.)*

EMORY. Oh, Rick's about to sing! I'd better get my act together.

*(EMORY runs up the stairs and into the bathroom, closing the door. Meanwhile, HAROLD goes to the terrace door, looks outside.)*

HAROLD. *( Re: group on the terrace.)* — Jesus! It looks like the United Colors of Benneton out there! *(To MICHAEL.)* Have you got Sitting Bull stashed in the closet?

HANK. Some of Larry's younger friends.

HAROLD. And a fine looking lot they are too. The white one's a serial killer, at the very least. And I thoroughly approve of him.

MICHAEL. Who was the bottle blond you were with at the service.

HAROLD. An actor-singer-dancer-waiter. Well, he's not really a dancer, but he moves. In fact he's moving into my apartment this very minute.

MICHAEL. What?!!

HAROLD. Just temporarily till he finds a place. I'm only trying to do my bit for the arts. He sent his regrets.

MICHAEL. I'm *distraught* that he couldn't come.

HAROLD. I knew you would be. He and I are making dinner at home tonight so I dare not eat a thing. In fact, I've got to lose twenty pounds by seven-thirty. — He's cute as a mouse's ear, dontcha think? *(Exits to terrace, expansively:)* Hello, boys, here's your Aunt Harold! Come cheer me up!

*(He glides outside, humming. Those left in his wake exchange looks. RICK can be heard singing a love song in French. The quality ought to have the bittersweet, nostalgic feeling of a classic French love song.*

*MICHAEL is left alone, moves towards the bar cabinet. He opens it. In the fading light, it seems even brighter, more sparkling, more seductive than before. RICK's voice continues outside....*

*The lights fade with only the bar light intensifying. Another moment ...*

*BLACKOUT.)*

## END OF ACT I

## ACT II

*(As the house lights fade, RICK's voice can be heard singing, accompanying himself on the guitar....)*
*As the lights come up on the stage, MICHAEL closes the bar cabinet, shutting off its light. Outside, on the terrace, RICK finishes up the French love song. This is followed by applause from all. MICHAEL slowly crosses to the terrace door.)*

HAROLD. *(Offstage.)* — Fabulous, Rickola! Or, should I say, "Fah-boo-*luzz*"! Now, let's hear a *Yankee* song! For us *Yanks*!
MICHAEL. *(At terrace door.)* That *was* a Yankee song, Harold! For us Yanks from New Orleans.

*(Thunder. Groans all around from everyone outside.)*

HAROLD. *(Offstage, comic Southern accent.)* — Well, ah declare, y'all, ah do believe we are about to have a spring *squall*.
BERNARD. *(Offstage, comic Southern accent.)* Sugah, you know a real good squallin' generally follows a heat wave — 'specially a *French* one!

*(There is a clap of thunder. Audible reactions from the group outside, followed by the sound of a sudden downpour.)*

MICHAEL. Just leave everything on the table under the awning and cover the casserole!

*(Much hooting as everyone dashes inside, most carrying their drinks, plates of food and smart cotton napkins, which they use to blot the raindrops. RICK hangs on to his guitar but waves an empty stem glass....)*

RICK. — Did anyone grab the champagne?
DONALD. *(Holds up Bombay bottle.)* I grabbed the champagne of bottled gins. First things first!
MICHAEL. *(To DONALD, disapprovingly.)* You *could* just start the day with a gin enema. Why fuck around and wait for things to take effect? *(To RICK re: champagne.)* There's a bottle of Cristal in the fridge. — *(Re: rainstorm.)* Somebody close the doors till it slackens a bit!
HAROLD. *(Blotting his brow.)* Maybe we ought to ask the super to come up and mop us off.

*(JASON slides the terrace doors shut. RICK puts his guitar back in its case.)*

JASON. *(To RICK.)* Rick, what's that song mean in plain English?
BERNARD. Yeah, what about us dumb bastards who didn't go to Le Rosey?

*(RICK strums the intro again and speaks the song in a loose translation of the French. RICK accompanies his oral recitation, delivered more briskly than the singing, with appropriate chords....)*

RICK. *(Speaking, not singing.)*
Tonight, the wind that beats on my door
Speaks to me of love that's lost
And I think of times gone by ...

What is there left of our love?
What is there left of happy days?
A photograph, an old photo
Of my youth ...

Of faded bliss,
Of wind-blown hair
A stolen kiss,
A dream we share —
What's left of this?
Can you tell me?
A memory, —

Letters you wrote that I still keep
Lines I can quote that make me weep
The rest is gone. Why is it gone?
Pourquoi?

*(More enthusiastic applause than before.)*

    MICHAEL. *(To BERNARD.)* You *do* comprehend "pourquoi," don't you?
    BERNARD. Yeah, it means "fuck *you*," doesn't it?

*(HANK crosses to RICK.)*

    HANK. *(Calmly, sincerely.)* That was terrific, Rick. Really. — Larry told you he liked that song?
    RICK. *(Carefully.)* — Yeah. *(Deeply appreciative.)* I'm glad *you* like it, Hank. I hoped you would.
    HANK. I did. Very, very much. Thank you.

*(RICK smiles at HANK, turns to go put his guitar in its case.)*

## THE MEN FROM THE BOYS

BERNARD. *(Looking about.)* Where the hell is Emmy?
HAROLD. — Who's next on the bill and what language is it in?

*(The bathroom door opens, EMORY quickly emerges and strikes a pose at the top of the stairs.)*

EMORY. *(Theatrically.)* *I'm* next! — And it's in the mother tongue! — For all you *mothers*.

*(Everyone looks up as a kind of vision descends the stairs. EMORY is completely (and wonderfully) made up: bright, glossy red lipstick, shaded cheekbones, dramatic eye shadow and thick false lashes. No wig, however, and no women's clothes. He has only put on the jacket to his black velour suit, turned up the lapels and buttoned it to the throat. Around his neck are several strands of sparkling rhinestones. Brilliant drops dangle from his ears, and on his wrists and fingers are dazzling bracelets and rings. He is carrying a cassette and a small camera.*
*Instant applause, hoots and whistles! EMORY goes to pop the cassette into the tape deck and deposit his camera on the étagère. There is a round of applause as everyone settles into chairs, upon the stairs or on the floor.)*

EMORY. *(A seasoned pro from the school of yesteryear.)* Thank you. Thank you, ladies and gentlemen — and you among you know who's who. — This next little ditty does not come from Paris or Pa*ree*, whichever you prefer. — Personally, I prefer New York! Yes, make mine Manhattan and make my day! *(Imperiously, to MICHAEL.)* — Michael, my *lights*. My *lights*!

*(MICHAEL goes to a wall switch as the intro on the tape begins. A hush falls over the room, MICHAEL hits the wall switch and EMORY stands in a lone pool of strategically*

*focused light.*
*The next exchanges are rapid volleys....)*

HAROLD. Oh, the Marlene keylight. Why didn't I have that for *my* entrance?!
EMORY. Check the cheekbones! —
BERNARD. Did you say chicken bones?
EMORY. *(Re: BERNARD.)* Oh, *kill her*! — *Cheek*bones! How're my *cheek*bones?
JASON. They look like Carlsbad Caverns.
EMORY. *(Playfully.)* — Well, that's not because of the light. That's because I had all my wisdom teeth extracted this afternoon. *(He sucks in his cheeks. Mild laughter. Campily, sultry.)* I come before you without wisdom. *(French pronunciation.)* — But with "cou*rage*."
HAROLD. Yeah, first comes "cou*rage*," then comes regret.
EMORY. *(American accent.)* Je ne regrette rien, she*ree*!

*(BERNARD sits on the stairs, gives a grandstand razz....)*

BERNARD. *(Through cupped hands.)* I hope your song's better 'n your material!
EMORY. *(To EMORY.)* Oh, you're *terrible*.
BERNARD. But you're fucking nuts about me!
DONALD. *(To BERNARD.)* Quiet in the bleachers!
JASON. Yeah, come on, guys, settle down! Shhh....

*(Everyone quiets. EMORY stands perfectly still in his "spotlight," sparkling with command.)*

EMORY. *(Over accompaniment.)* — Larry always spoke up for freedom. Freedom to be yourself, with no need to lie or pretend. This song is for Larry. —

## 58 THE MEN FROM THE BOYS

*(The taped intro ends and the accompaniment begins. EMORY sings/ speaks a song entitled "I'm Not the Man I Planned." What follows is a suggestion of what the "flavor" ought to be — particularly its bawdy music hall/burlesque house tone. [See page 92 for sheet music.])*

EMORY. *(Sings/speaks.)*
I'm not the man I planned:
A life I'd founded on fam'ly aesthetics
A wife surrounded with kids and athletics
Instead I astounded the town with cosmetics.
My structure faltered —
My foundation altered —
An' I'm not the man I planned.

I'm not the guy I dreamed
The square in conventional coats and ties.
Though I still wear suits, now I mesmerize
Simply because I accessorize.

*(He whips a red ostrich fan from under his jacket, snaps it open and fans himself.)*

With plumage I pepped up
With high high heels I schlepped up
And I'm not the guy I dreamed! —

Now it's a cinch
I'm gay as a finch!
And I tell you without much ado —
I'm such a queer *bird*
That maybe you've *heard*
I'd never love a dove,
But I'd kiss a cockatoo!

*(Singing.)*
I'm no longer boring and bland
A dead-on-arrival fashion victim.
Now I'm archival, and this is my dictum:
Provincial drag is an outmoded mess
Come to New York 'n cross dress for success.
I divested in transis
Got arrested in Kansas ...
But I shout "Eureka and encore!"
I'm not in Topeka anymore!
And thank God not the clod I planned.

*(Applause and whistles. EMORY bows graciously, a geisha shielding half his face behind his fan. The noise dies down....)*

MICHAEL. How many musical interludes are there going to be?
HAROLD. Well, I hope it's not like what they used to say about films from India — "If it's serious, there are only *ten* numbers." — Just kidding, Em, you were heaven!
EMORY. *(To HAROLD.)* That was the second and *last* number, thank you very much! — I always close the bill! The musical portion, anyhow. —
MICHAEL. *(To the group.)* Now, anybody who has something to say can say it. —

*(There is some low mumbling among the group, but no one stands immediately....)*

EMORY. *(Low hiss.)* — Bernard! — Bernard! — Say something.

*(EMORY crosses to the étagère to put away his fan and get his camera. BERNARD stands, clears his throat as EMORY goes to*

*sit on the stairs unobtrusively.)*

BERNARD. *(To the group.)* — The last time I went to see Larry in the hospital, he said a funny thing to me — because no matter what spiritual fad he was into, he really thought organized religion was destructive and just caused trouble between people. So I was surprised when he said, "After I'm gone will you do me a favor? Will you go in a church and light a candle for me?" And, of course, I didn't question him, I just said I would. But then, in typical Larry fashion he added: "Not just *any* old church but someplace like that one you see across the street when you come out of the Fiftieth Street side door of Sak's Fifth Avenue." — That was Larry.

*(Applause. BERNARD sits down as HAROLD goes to the étagère and picks up the photograph of Larry....)*

HAROLD. Has everyone seen this wonderful picture of Lair"? Hank took it on the beach in Brazil. *(HAROLD hands it to the person nearest him and it is passed hand-to-hand in a circle until it is seen by all and returned to him. Meanwhile ...to HANK.)* How long ago?
HANK. I swear I can't remember.
JASON. *(Coolly.)* It'll be three years this summer.
RICK. That's a great straw hat. He had style.
EMORY. In fact, sometimes he was style *heavy*. Remember the summer when he bought fish bowls from Pier One for white wine glasses?
DONALD. *(Nostalgically.)* And we never had to get up to freshen our drinks.
BERNARD. And when we *had* to get up, we *couldn't*.

*(Laughter from the old-timers, especially DONALD. RICK and JASON don't find it funny, and BERNARD's smile fades with realization....)*

## THE MEN FROM THE BOYS 61

BERNARD. Gives me the shakes just thinking about it.
MICHAEL. *("Absently.")* Me, too.
EMORY. *(To RICK.)* That was back when we smoked and drank and there were no gyms and restaurants cooked with grease.
HAROLD. Yeah, and the baths were great for Emergency Love.
MICHAEL. Yeah, and I hated myself for being gay. Then I came out, and *other* people hated me.
JASON. The dark ages.

*(Laughter.)*

EMORY. Yeah. Now the world's enlightened and in a holding pattern. *I'm* in a holding pattern. Well, I know my *looks* are in a holding pattern. — Now, who's gonna say something?

*(There is a moment of mumbling as everyone wonders who's going to be the next person to speak. JASON stands and the group quiets as HAROLD replaces the picture on the étagère....)*

JASON. *(To the group.)* — It was not in Larry's nature to be somber or self-pitying, so I'm going to do my best to be like him. We, in this room, are Larry's "family." Each of us was sort of a different relative, with a different sort of relationship. Each of us may know something about him the others do not, but each of us knows what the other has lost. I think it's his honesty I'll remember most — more than his wit or his charm or his ageless good looks. *(A round of applause. Shifting gears.)* — Larry loved life and lived it by his own code. There was an edge to everything he believed or said, whether it was smart-ass or serious. He had his own standards and refused to live by ....
MICHAEL. Where's this going?
JASON. — Larry believed that men with men — and women with women — are a completely different human dynamic from men

with women and women with men. —

MICHAEL. *(Overlapping.)* Are you coming to the point? ...

BERNARD. *(Calmly.)* Michael, let Jason say what he wants to say.

EMORY. Yeah.

JASON. *(Pressing on.)* — For Larry, the fight for legalized gay marriage was about protection: tax exemptions, benefits, inheritances ....

MICHAEL. *Now, wait just a minute!*

DONALD. *Michael*!

JASON. *(Accelerating, overlapping.)* — Basically being fed-up with gays getting screwed out of what any spouse who had a piece of paper would be entitled to! —

MICHAEL. *(Interrupting.)* Listen, *posterboy*, this is not a pep rally nor a protest! You are *not* on a platform *nor* a soapbox, you are in *my* living room and I will not have you haranguing or handcuffing yourself to the Biedermeier!

*(HANK stands.)*

HANK. *(With authority.)* That's really enough out of the two of you! *(The room immediately quiets. Coolly.)* Jason, you're right about Larry, but you *are* a bit off the track. And Michael, as usual, you're just *out of line.*

MICHAEL. *(Thinks, sighs.)* — Of course I am. I apologize.

JASON. So do I.

HAROLD. *(After a moment.)* Thanks, Hank. I was hoping someone would kick them *both* in the nuts.

MICHAEL. *(Sarcastically.)* What do you want to be when *you* grow up, Harold?

HAROLD. Broadminded.

HANK. *(After a moment.)* Yes. Broadminded. Larry greatly appreciated the "differentness" of being gay. So he didn't want to ape heterosexual conventions — particularly marital ones. Larry knew that a real bond between us had nothing to do with a piece of paper — that it was only important that he and I be married in our minds. He knew being wed had nothing to do with legality — only to do with the personal, private, unique contract between two consenting grownups. And the ground rules you make yourself. And they can't be the same for all. — Maybe it's only now that I can say something to him ... to *myself*: that through it all — faithfulness, fear, infidelity, forgiveness — our *marriage* was never threatened. We were together a long time on our own terms.

JASON. Hear, hear!
MICHAEL. *(To JASON.)* Will you shut the fuck up?!
DONALD. Michael, please!
MICHAEL. Oh, all right! Cut my throat. See if *I* care.
EMORY. — Let's all raise our glasses in a final toast. — *(Everyone stands, raises his glass, no matter what it contains, wine or water....)* To Larry. Peaceful at last. *(Everyone drinks. HANK goes over to JASON and puts his arms around him to hug him for a long moment. RICK watches closely. EMORY waves his camera.)* Photo op! Photo op!
HAROLD. *(Covers his face with EMORY's fan.)* No pictures, *please*!
MICHAEL. *(With disgust.)* Snapshots?! Ugh!!
EMORY. Hush! — Both of you! *(Corralling the group.)* Now, don't everybody break up! Move in! Move in!
BERNARD. Come on, Michael! Come on, you guys! Bunch up!
DONALD. Orgy time!
HAROLD. — If only.

*(The group starts to assemble opposite the stairs.)*

RICK. *(To EMORY.)* You're the one that ought to be in the picture!

EMORY. Don't worry!

*(He snaps a timing button, sets the camera on an eye-level rung of the stairs and rushes toward the center of the group. He lunges into a rope of interwoven arms and is bounced back to his feet, like a dazed, bejeweled prizefighter. He grabs RICK and JASON around their necks and holds on as the group lets out a raucous "Whooaahhh!")*

HAROLD. *(Quickly.)* Might know you'd take center stage!
EMORY. *(Quickly.)* Shut up and lick your lips!
BERNARD. *Hold* it, everybody!
EMORY. — And say, "Lesbian!"
THE ENTIRE GROUP. *(Unison, producing frozen smiles.) LESBIAN!!*

*(The flash goes off! A cheer goes up! EMORY rushes back to the camera, the group disperses. RICK slides open the terrace doors, goes outside.)*

BERNARD. *(To MICHAEL.)* What happened to Scott?
MICHAEL. *(Coolly.)* He had to go. He asked me to say his goodbyes.
HAROLD. I never even got a chance to say *hello*!
EMORY. And I'm sure you're heartbroken.
HAROLD. *(Feigning naiveté.)* Why, whatever do you mean?

*(RICK enters from the terrace with the bottle of champagne.)*

JASON. Yeah, what *do* you mean, Harold?
EMORY. Hallie doesn't care for the boy.
HAROLD. Scott is an acquired taste — which I have somehow failed to acquire. *(Bluntly, to EMORY.)* No, I don't. And you don't either.

## THE MEN FROM THE BOYS

EMORY. And neither does Bernard.
BERNARD. I've never said a word against Scott!
EMORY. *(To BERNARD.)* But you don't like him. I can tell. — Larry liked him, I guess.
HAROLD. Larry just liked to *look* at him.
HANK. No, Larry *liked* him. He thought someone would be good for Michael.

*(A pause. RICK pours himself a flute of champagne, listens with interest.)*

JASON. — Scott's really kind of crazy. I mean like nuts. Really.
EMORY. Well, who isn't a little. *(Gestures with one hand.)* I'm schizophrenic. *(Gestures with the other.)* — And so am *I*!
JASON. *(Continuing.)* I found that out when I sold him my bike.

*(MICHAEL eyes JASON suspiciously.)*

HAROLD. *(Bluntly, to JASON; for MICHAEL's benefit.)* Scott's a crawler. And an opportunist.
MICHAEL. Don't hold back, Harold.
JASON. It's the crystal that makes him crazy.
MICHAEL. *(Seething.)* How would you know that?!
JASON. When he came to our apartment to pick up the bike, his eyelids were on the ceiling. He sat on the floor for four hours playing video games and didn't blink once. — My boyfriend knows his dealer.
BERNARD. I thought he was clean.
JASON. That's *his* story.
MICHAEL. *(Snaps.)* Scott does not lie!
JASON. *(To MICHAEL, flatly.)* Scott's the kind of guy who steals your drugs and then helps you look for them!

*(DONALD freshens his drink with gin.)*

DONALD. *(To MICHAEL.)* You don't know when he's lying and when he isn't.

RICK. He must tell the truth sometimes.

HAROLD. Only when his imagination flags.

MICHAEL. *( To all,* seriously *factitious.)* Scott is just a welcome antidote to heartiness.

*(RICK takes his guitar case upstairs.)*

DONALD. He uses you, Michael. He plays you like a violin.

EMORY. He couldn't. Michael had all his old violins made into shoe trees.

HAROLD. Scott has made *Michael* into a shoe tree. It's one thing to get fucked. It's another to get fucked *over.*

MICHAEL. *(For DONALD's benefit.)* None of us ever likes any of our so-called "other" friends.

HANK. — I like everybody and everybody's friends. Everybody here, I mean. *My* friends and *their* friends. —

MICHAEL. That's because you're not a cunt, Hank.

DONALD. We all get rattled when we show up with a new trick, or a twinkie.

MICHAEL. Scott is neither a *trick* nor a *twinkie*, thank you very much!

EMORY. I guess you struck a nerve, Donald.

HAROLD. I think it was Jason who did the root canal.

RICK. *(Coming downstairs.)* Is that how you think of us? That we're nothing but cheap tricks?

JASON. *(To RICK.)* Speak for yourself.

RICK. — I *am* speaking for myself. *(To group.)* — But, God, how could anybody's younger friends stand up next to you guys?

JASON. *(Drolly.)* You mean for honesty and loyalty and charity?

RICK. I mean for *longevity.*

EMORY. Longevity?! You're not talking about old fucking

redwoods again, are you?!

RICK. Longevity of friendship.

EMORY. I'll have you know I'm still in my deep forties.

BERNARD. If you're fortysomething, this must be your second time on earth!

DONALD. *(To RICK.)* It's been a longer run for some of us than for others.

BERNARD. We do resent each other's "other friends." For once, you're absolutely right, Michael. We're proprietous as hell about one another. We're a closed corporation. We don't like anybody else. How could we, when we can barely stand each other?

EMORY. Don't be sil, we *adore* each other.

JASON. *(Sardonically.)* Oh, yeah, sure you do!

BERNARD. We do! — We just don't like outsiders. And not just you. — *(To EMORY.)* How do you *really* feel about my wife?

EMORY. I *adore* your wife! How can you ask such a question? Women are not threats to gay men. "Other women." I don't know why. It's strange, but any guy I was ever interested in could have had all the girlfriends he wanted — just not boyfriends. We just get nervous to a degree when some one of us shows up with a twinkie. *(Sees MICHAEL glaring.)* — Eh ... a recruit.

BERNARD. You wouldn't know what a real recruit was if you fell over one. I doubt if you know what the words "military service" mean.

EMORY. For your information, I've fallen for my share of recruits and serviced the military quite patriotically! — Oh, Mary, don't ask and *don't tell*!

JASON. Do you have a patent on camp?

EMORY. *(To JASON, cuttingly.)* Yeah, it's a *black* patent, sweetie! — Some of us were more outrageous *before* Stonewall! Some of us were just as in-your-face as *you* ever hoped to be!

JASON. Flaming with resentment?

EMORY. *(With an edge.)* We were funny, dear. *(Looks over the group; pointedly.)* Now, there're not so many of us left.

JASON. *(Re: EMORY's kind.)* Mmm, you're an endangered species!

EMORY. *(Tough.)* Listen, kiddo, before there were marches, there was a band.

JASON. *(To EMORY.)* And you were in the front line, were you? — Well, congratulations.

EMORY. You don't have to get all Dorothy Darling with me now. I just happened to be walking by, minding my own business. Wearing a dress, of course, but minding my own business.

MICHAEL. Just out for the evening, trawling for love.

EMORY. We weren't just lifestyles *that* night, we were news!

MICHAEL. *(Aside, to JASON.)* Stay off those floats! It's bad PR! *(Considering JASON.)* — A parade with three hundred thousand people in attendance and the TV news has to focus on ten people in leather and chains and three of the ugliest drags known to man!

EMORY. Well, Stonewall changed my life. In fact, it brought me *to* life. It brought my hidden talents into a follow spot. I used to have to pay to get out of jail for doing what I *get paid* to do now!

RICK. I admire what you did. It took guts.

JASON. You may not be into leather or drag, Michael. You may not approve. But, like it or not, it's part of the real world.

DONALD. The public wants *theatre*! Not dentists in their double-knit suits.

JASON. Yeah, if you want the boy next door, go next door.

EMORY. Didn't Joan Crawford say that?

MICHAEL. No, she said, "Just who is kidding *whom*."

*(Mild laughter. Suddenly, RICK speaks....)*

RICK. — I lie too. About who I am and what I am.

MICHAEL. What are you talking about.

RICK. Well ... I'm not Vietnamese-American. My father wasn't an officer in the military. My mother didn't speak French. I just took a course at the Alli*ance*. — I'm Filipino.

HAROLD. So?

RICK. *(Calmly.)* So I've lied about who I am all my adult life.

HANK. Why?

RICK. I always wanted to be BEYOND Polynesian, I wanted to be more "high born." More "aristocratic." — Do you know what the second largest population in Hong Kong is — after Americans? Filipino workers. Filipino *domestic* workers.

BERNARD. When it comes to domestic workers, what do you think about *my* people?

EMORY. You've never denied your background, Bernard.

BERNARD. I guess we all wonder just how honest we've been with ourselves. How much we've denied. — I wish I could be more like Larry in that department. More upfront, no matter what. *(Reflectively.)* — When I was a kid in Grosse Pointe, there used to be a Chinese couple — who worked for the same family my mother did, the Dahlbecks. And their oldest kid, the son, used to refer to them behind their backs as "The Slits." And when he did, I used to laugh. God only knows what he said behind *my* back about *me*. *(Laughs bitterly at thought.)* — I wonder if he used to laugh that way about the little colored hypocrite who had a crush on him. *(After a moment.)* — I went home last Christmas to see my mother. While I was there, I stopped to say hello to him. He sold the big house and now lives alone in a big condo but still has two servants who live in.

JASON. *Two* servants! How can two people have a full-time job, working for just one guy? What's there to do?

BERNARD. Dust. Answer the phone. Take the abuse.

RICK. *(Sardonically.)* Oh, well, *that's* always a full-time job.

BERNARD. Yeah, in some people's lives that's a *career*! — Peter's a bitter and difficult old man now.

HANK. You think he's gay?

BERNARD. No, not at all.

EMORY. He couldn't be. Bernard described his furniture.

RICK. *(Reflectively.)* — There's even discrimination within the gay community: a bouncer just assumed my cock wasn't big enough to get into a leather bar. So he didn't let me in. God only knows what *he* was.

HAROLD. A bastard for sure.

RICK. — I've thought about plastic surgery — you know, "westernize" my eyes.

HAROLD. — I'd trade places with you just as you are. — Oh, to have your skin. Oh, just to be your age — *with* your skin! I understand the contempt this country feels for the old. Getting old is the greatest sin in America. Worse than dying poor. *(Looks at JASON.)* — And why not, as long as Calvin Klein continues to make us feel awful about ourselves? But since we're no longer in hiding and it appears that we're going to live, what are we going to *do* with ourselves?

EMORY. — It's not easy when you're asked to leave the dance floor. Why was it that with Larry, his age didn't seem to matter?

HAROLD. It did sometimes. And when it did, it hurt. It just didn't matter to everyone. *(Smiles at HANK; to EMORY.)* — Larry was handsome and you are not. Nor is Michael. Nor am I.

MICHAEL. Harold, you have an *obsession* with beauty. You always have.

JASON. *(Tauntingly.)* You got something against beauty, Michael?

HAROLD. *(Coolly.)* Thanks, Jason, but I can bridge this gap myself. — One, Michael, I'm an American. And, two, I'm human. And three, I don't *lie* about such things. People don't want anything ugly. Clothes or cars or whatever. Of course, they may choose something that's fucking hideous or tacky or tasteless to others, but to them, you can bet it's beautiful. It's sexy! It sings! It *sells*! *(Reflectively.)* — The beauties of the world can never know us. And we can never know them. Because they never, ever have to deal with the nature of our agony in coming to grips with our baggage. Every day we are banking the fires. They live a life sustained in an oblivious, effortless, cozy glow — being worshiped, and adored, and catered to. — Being ... *wanted.*

RICK. *("In-the-know" non sequitur.)* Older gay men want younger men — just like older straight men want younger women.

BERNARD. And older women want good-looking young guys.

HAROLD. Well, love is one thing. Getting your pulse jump-started is another.

RICK. Yeah.

HAROLD. *(After a moment.)* My outside has never reflected what's inside my brain, my aesthetic sense of myself. When I look in the mirror I do not see what I see in my mind's eye. I have never liked anything that fails to please me visually — including my own looks. I don't want to *have* Brad Pitt — I want to *look like* Brad Pitt. Anybody who says exteriors don't matter is full of shit. — And you can quote me. Fulsomely.

JASON. *(Looking outside.)* The rain has stopped.

EMORY. *(Generally.)* En voiture!

*(Everyone starts to shift, stretch, make noise ....)*

HANK. Could I say one quick thing before we break up? —

BERNARD. Hang on, everyone! —

*(The room quiets....)*

HANK. — We'll go out of here, and all of this will be forgotten. But no matter, this was *done* for him. And for *us.* — What we take away from here — the difference in the way we feel ... and aren't even yet aware of — that's what this was about. — Thank you all for being here. And thank you for not having asked all the wrong questions.

*(A final round of applause as JASON slides open the terrace doors.)*

RICK. *(Re: weather.)* It's gonna be a nice day after all!

*(Everyone begins to break up and move. HAROLD goes to JASON, says a silent goodbye. RICK shakes hands with HANK ....)*

BERNARD. *(To EMORY.)* You're not walking out of here with me looking like the eleventh-best dressed woman!
EMORY. — This is *not* my daytime look.
BERNARD. Well, get on your "Daytime *Traveling* Look" and hurry up about it!
EMORY. I won't be a minute! Don't get in a tiz! I've just gotta tissue off my base and find my petit point.

*(EMORY turns for the stairs. HAROLD and JASON finish their silent "goodbyes," JASON reaches for his cigarettes, takes out one, lights up and goes outside. MICHAEL furiously fans the smoke in his wake. HAROLD stops EMORY at the base of the stairs....)*

HAROLD. *(To MICHAEL.)* I hate to dine and dash, but I've got to get back to my blond houseguest.
MICHAEL. *(Still fanning smoke.)* Why rush?! You might be on *time*!
EMORY. Now, now, you two. We've already had dinner and a show. —
HAROLD. *(To EMORY.)* Gimme a kiss, puppy.
EMORY. *(Kisses HAROLD on cheek, hurries up the stairs.)* — I wanna hear how it works out. *All* the lurid details.
HAROLD. *(To EMORY.)* I'll call you and give you a blow by blow account — oh, catch me, Dr. Freud, I'm slipping! —

*(HAROLD hugs HANK, turns away. He picks up his rain cape and*

## THE MEN FROM THE BOYS

*umbrella.*
*EMORY runs upstairs, peels off his eyelashes as he enters the bathroom.)*

BERNARD. Bye, Hallie.
HAROLD. *(To BERNARD.)* Bye, love. — Now, I don't want you cheating on your wife while she's out of town on an errand of mercy. *(Dryly.)* — Donald. We've got to stop meeting like this.
DONALD. Yeah, Harold, ain't it the truth.
HAROLD. — You think I'm kidding!

*(DONALD shakes his head, moves away. JASON turns to BERNARD.)*

JASON. *(To BERNARD.)* Will you help me bring in the bar cart?
BERNARD. Yeah, and it won't even send me into the well-known "downward spiral."

*(BERNARD follows JASON; they exit to the terrace.)*

RICK. — Nice to see you Harold.
HAROLD. Sayonara, Ricky. Sorry I can't say it in Tagalog. We should visit your homeland together — I'm mad to do the Pacific Rim. — If you're ever in the Village, I'm in the book.
RICK. Don't be surprised if you hear from me.
HAROLD. Young man, nothing surprises *me*.
RICK. Michael, what'd you do with the rest of the raincoats?
MICHAEL. Hung 'em on the shower door.

*(RICK goes upstairs.)*

HAROLD. *(To MICHAEL.)* Let's talk sometime within the next eighteen-hour window.

MICHAEL. Get out of here!

*(They air-kiss on both cheeks.)*

HAROLD. Constant touch. Missing you already!

*(HAROLD whips on his cape with a great flourish and is out the door. JASON and BERNARD lift the bar cart over the terrace door jamb. HANK puts on his coat. RICK lingers at the top of the stairs, looking down at HANK.)*

BERNARD. *(To HANK.)* How are you getting home?
HANK. Subway, I guess.
BERNARD. We'll share a cab and drop you off.
HANK. Thanks, but I'm way out of your way. Besides, I really want to be by myself.

*(BERNARD nods.)*

DONALD. So long, Hank....
HANK. Donald. —

*(They hug, DONALD turns back to the bar cart, takes the silver casserole chafing dish off the cart and into the kitchen.)*

BERNARD. *(Loudly toward upstairs.)* Let's *GO*, Emory! — Thanks, Michael. I apologize if I lost it there for moment.
MICHAEL. Amends are not necessary, Bernard. You know I appreciate your concern. — Bye the way, are *you* still in therapy?
BERNARD. Just low maintenance. — Ciao, baby! Don't say it *ain't* been!

*(They kiss on the check. BERNARD turns to HANK and they silently*

## THE MEN FROM THE BOYS

*and fondly hug each other. EMORY comes out of the bathroom, heads downstairs carrying his small makeup case, his face cleaned. RICK enters the bathroom, closes the door.)*

EMORY. *(To MICHAEL.)* — Listen, she*ree*, it's been seamless. Absolutely seamless. When I go, I'd like to have a celebration exactly like this one.
MICHAEL. We have next Thursday open.
EMORY. Oh, that hurt worse than a slap with a suede glove! *(He crosses to kiss HANK on the cheek. Blows MICHAEL a kiss.)* Bye, dear. Stay pretty.

*(BERNARD shakes his head as he and EMORY are out the front door.)*

HANK. Some assortment, this group!
MICHAEL. Like a cheap box of chocolates. Some dark, some white. — Even an exotic honey-dipped confection.
HANK. *(Reflectively.)* Some soft, some brittle. —
MICHAEL. *(Pleasantly.)* And all either too sweet or too *bitter*sweet. And that includes this old bonbon.
HANK. But we change whether we like it or not.
MICHAEL. You mean we get *older* whether we like it or not.
HANK. No, I mean we change. Change *is* possible. Growth *is* possible. I believe that, Michael.
MICHAEL. Some people change. Some people never change. Some just sit on the fence. I don't think we ever quite shake-off whatever it is we settle on being somewhere around the age of three. It's all over by then. *I* believe that.
HANK. *(Salutes MICHAEL with his stemmed glass.)* Theorize, and drink champagne.

*(HANK drains his glass.)*

MICHAEL. Listen, you don't think I've had *too much* analysis, do you? Or gone a step too far? Like, *thirteen*. You know how I always overdo everything.

HANK. Well, none of it did you any harm. It couldn't have. It was either that or die.

MICHAEL. — Hank, I've never told you how much I admire the way you dealt with Larry's extracurricular activities. —

HANK. It may have been a marriage of now and then untrue bodies, but it was one of constantly true minds. — Messy. Like life. *(Changes subject.)* — Listen, there isn't any possible way to say ....

MICHAEL. *(Cuts him off, quietly.)* No. Don't. Please.

HANK. I'm not. Not *now*. I'm going to write my feelings down and send them to you — and I know that's risky with a writer, but it's what I want to do.

MICHAEL. Oh, Hank —— have no fear. — I want to thank *you*. I won't forget this afternoon. For many reasons.

*(MICHAEL and HANK embrace and part. MICHAEL opens the door for HANK, who goes out. MICHAEL closes the door as JASON enters from the terrace.)*

JASON. Everybody gone?

MICHAEL. Well, the tide's not *completely* out.

JASON. Why do you dislike me so? I don't think it's my politics. I actually think we're on the same side.

MICHAEL. The only thing we share is our anger.

JASON. One outwardly, one inwardly. You know, you might be useful if you were going in the right direction.

MICHAEL. Don't patronize me.

JASON. Hardly. Your contentment, your complacency may have allowed *you* to survive, but they won't get *me* through. I've got to do something about the way things are.

MICHAEL. You dismiss us — me and my kind — and worse yet, you make us responsible for everything you take for granted! How do you think you got it?

JASON. Well, you and your cronies have sadly outlived your purpose.

MICHAEL. So you'd be just as glad if we didn't exist. We're in your way.

JASON. That's right. You're expendable.

MICHAEL. Listen, Jason, if it weren't for boys like us, there wouldn't be men like you.

JASON. Now who's being patronizing?

MICHAEL. *(Bluntly.)* — You're the one who stole Scott's bike, aren't you?

JASON. What?

MICHAEL. You did drugs with him, and he passed out, and you took his bike, probably thinking it was yours.

JASON. Michael, I don't do drugs, and I'm not a thief. I take an oath on my life — on my lover's life!

MICHAEL. If I didn't like you before, now I really have no use for you.

JASON. Well, if you won't listen to reason. —

*(JASON starts to leave.)*

MICHAEL. *(Softer tone.)* Wait! — I *will* listen to reason.

JASON. *(Stops and turns.)* I sold him my old bike, which, I assume, was paid for with your money. He came by to look at it, said he'd think it over, and left. Half an hour later he called and said he'd take it. When I took it by his place, he asked if I'd like to do some "K" with him and go dancing, but I said no. I left the bike with him and left him alone. I'm not lying.

*(DONALD enters from the kitchen.)*

DONALD. *(To JASON.)* Are you staying in the city or going back to the Hamptons?

JASON. I'm going back. *(Puts on raincoat.)* But I have to stop and pick up the mail and get a sweater. It's colder on the island than I thought. Why — you want to get the jitney together? Or take a train?

DONALD. I drove into town. My car's in a garage between First and Second. I don't mind waiting, if you don't mind driving. I've had a little more to drink than I thought.

JASON. I don't mind at all!

DONALD. — You ought to come over to my place. I have a fire almost every evening. And I have lots of sweaters you're welcome to. — Not as many as Michael, of course.

JASON. I wouldn't want to go in Michael's sweater closet for fear of being killed by falling Missonis.

*(DONALD laughs a little drunkenly. MICHAEL is slightly disturbed by DONALD's condition.)*

DONALD. *(To MICHAEL, drolly.)* I washed the stemware by hand.

MICHAEL. You don't still do windows, do you?

DONALD. Thanks … for the memories.

MICHAEL. Say no more.

DONALD. Where's *my* coat?

*(DONALD stumbles on the rung of the stairs.)*

MICHAEL. *(Sotto to JASON, caringly.)* Will you … uh … will you be sure that he ….

JASON. *(Nods; sotto.)* Yeah, yeah, sure.

DONALD. *(Turns to them with dignity.)* Surely, I'm not the first person you've every seen fall *up* the stairs.

MICHAEL. Donald, I don't think you *had* a coat. Take one of mine if you like. — *(Dryly.)* And there's no danger of avalanche. You don't have to hazard the Missoni section for the rain gear.

DONALD. *I had a blazer.* — I know I could find it if it had hair around it.

JASON. *(Picks up DONALD's blazer.)* Here it is.

*(DONALD crosses to JASON, who helps him on with his jacket.)*

DONALD. Thank you, dear boy.

JASON. So you're in real estate? *(DONALD nods.)* — You think a good bar and deli would go out there?

DONALD. *(Friendly.)* We'll do some pub crawling and see what's on its last legs. I know them all. I've long considered writing a book: *The Alcoholic's Guide to the Hamptons.* Not only furnish a complete listing of the best bars, but also have a vital statistics page with all the bar *orbits*, that is, *celebrations* of bars that've died during the year.

JASON. Sounds great. — I've been a flight attendant, a host in a restaurant, and, of course, a bartender. I think I could make a go of it with a place of my own. I'm good with the public.

DONALD. I can see why — you have charm. Not an easy thing to come by.

JASON. *(Smiles.)* — It's still raining pretty hard. Why don't you give me the ticket for your car and wait here. I'll be right back for you.

DONALD. *(Hands over ticket.)* With the greatest of pleasure. — No need to come up, just buzz and I'll go down.

JASON. — And maybe have a cup of coffee in the meantime. *(For MICHAEL's benefit.)* There's plenty left in that nice, simple pot.

*(DONALD laughs at MICHAEL's annoyance. JASON goes out the front door.)*

MICHAEL. *(To DONALD.)* Well, that's the last you'll see of him *or* that vulgar Lincoln Continental.

DONALD. *(Crosses to MICHAEL.)* — Tell me the truth, Michael, you miss it, don't you?

MICHAEL. On occasion, yes. On a nice occasion — like today or a birthday or New Year's — something clear and chilled to perfection doesn't seem half bad. Yes, Donald, I miss that fine, cozy, boozy feeling when it was at its best. But it's not possible. I'm a drunk, and I can't drink. Ever, ever again.

DONALD. Pity. *(Smiles.)* — It was a very nice afternoon, Michael. And we got through it without ever using the word "dysfunctional." It was just what Larry would have liked. Done just the way he could have liked it, with just the people he liked.

MICHAEL. *(Tongue-in-cheek, re: his expensive wristwatch.)* You know, I like my Cartier watch better than any of those people I invited this afternoon. — And I *don't* have a Rolex, no matter what your new boyfriend says.

DONALD. Didn't you hear Jason, he already has a lover.

MICHAEL. *(Looks at his Cartier.)* Yeah, they ought to be half way to Key West by now.

DONALD. *(Lightly.)* Michael, I trust him. *(Laughs feebly.)* — Once upon a time I'd have had a chance with someone like Jason. But, these days, I hardly stack-up to Larry, but … I must have something he's interested in.

MICHAEL. I don't think it's your mind — *or* your body.

DONALD. Well, if he thinks I'm rich, he's in for an epiphany. I'm just cozy. And I can be helpful to him. And who knows, maybe he does *like* older guys. He liked Larry. *(With meaning.)* — Some other young men did, too.

MICHAEL. *(Oblivious.)* I guess I was just always so goddamned jealous of Larry. Of his looks. Of his body. How he seemed to be blessed. How even his *toes* were beautiful. Of how he seemed to get every guy he ever wanted. Of how he and Hank seemed to beat the

## THE MEN FROM THE BOYS

odds and stay together.

DONALD. — You know, if you read Christopher Isherwood's diaries, you really wake-up to find out nothing for nobody is ever easy in life.

MICHAEL. You know, Donald, you're not the only one who can recite the alphabet! Isherwood and his partner, Don Bachardy, were always my ideal couple. But I was stunned to learn their relationship wasn't what I thought it was. Not what I thought I'd *missed*. You must think it absurd that I was shocked to find out ....

DONALD. To find out that they were human, too?

MICHAEL. Yeah, I guess so.

DONALD. Nobody has it all, Michael. Each of us has a lot to survive. Nobody escapes.

MICHAEL. Yeah. Not even beautiful Larry. — It's a shame to never have made a success of love with someone. But it just doesn't work for me. It can work for others. In fact, for others, it's essential. But it just can't work for me. It never has. For me, it's always been better to travel hopefully, then to ever arrive.

*(The downstairs door buzzes.)*

DONALD. *(Facetiously.)* That would be my car and driver. Or should I say, my *designated* driver.

MICHAEL. You worry me, Donald. — Be careful.

DONALD. You've mellowed, Michael. And that's to your credit. But don't every lose your anger. Without that, you're a living dead man. Not a vampire. Something worse.

MICHAEL. I know. I know. — Now, listen, keep your hands to yourself on the L.I.E. I don't want you dead in a car crash — even when you're *not* driving.

DONALD. Yessir. — *(Lightly.)* — To be continued. —

*(They hug and DONALD exits silently. MICHAEL closes the door as*

*RICK comes out of the bathroom and down they stairs.)*

RICK. — I hope you don't mind, I opened one of those little bars of soap, Michael. Like I couldn't resist the label.
MICHAEL. That's what they're there for.
RICK. Thanks. — Nice hand towels, too. French?
MICHAEL. Italian. — Thank *you* for the song. Maybe you ought to consider a really sensible career move like show business.
RICK. I've got other ideas — all thanks to Larry.
MICHAEL. Good on you, as the Australians say.

*(RICK goes to the door, turns to MICHAEL.)*

RICK. By the way, I couldn't help overhearing.... Jason was telling you the truth. He didn't take Scott's bike — *I* did.
MICHAEL. *You.*
RICK. It was my first time to do crystal and I never want to do it again. Honestly. That's definitely not my scene. — But I just couldn't resist the temptation, the curiosity. — So we went to his place.
MICHAEL. Why did you take his bike?
RICK. It can't explain it. It was crazy. I was speeding — and in a hurry on top of it. Scott was in the shower, and the bike was by the door and I just took it. But I took it *back*! I didn't *want it*! I didn't even remember where he lived. I had to ask Larry.
MICHAEL. Did you have sex with Scott too?
RICK. I wasn't interested.
MICHAEL. You knew Scott before today? You met him at the hospital at night?

*(RICK nods.)*

MICHAEL. *(Shocked.)* He never told me he went there without me.

RICK. Maybe like Larry, he kept his friends compartmentalized too.

MICHAEL. I guess he *did*.

RICK. At first, I though that he was Larry's lover, but then I began to see Hank and found out the story.

MICHAEL. Funny, I'd never even considered it — Scott and Larry.

RICK. I don't really know if they'd ever had a thing or not. I doubt it. Scott never said so.

MICHAEL. The two of you talked about it?

RICK. *(Nods.)* The night we did drugs. — The night I "borrowed" his bike.

MICHAEL. *(Incredulous.)* But you didn't even say hello to each other today.

RICK. I said "Hi" to him outside. He didn't want you to know we knew each other — or why.

MICHAEL. Scott still isn't aware you're the one?

RICK. *(Shakes his head.)* I never had a chance to explain.

MICHAEL. — You don't think Larry and Scott had a thing, do you?

RICK. *(Shakes head.)* I just think Larry was a soft touch.

MICHAEL. Scott asked him for money.

RICK. He just told him what a hard time he was having making it through school, and Larry felt sorry for him. Frankly, I think Scott just wanted it to buy drugs.

*(Suddenly, the door buzzes. MICHAEL goes to the wall panel, pushes the downstairs release.)*

MICHAEL. — Goodbye, Rick.

RICK. I hope we see each other again sometime.

MICHAEL. Yes … yes, of course.

*(RICK pulls on his coat. The apartment bell rings.)*

MICHAEL. *Now what*?!

*(MICHAEL opens the door.)*

MICHAEL. *(Surprised.)* Hank! What's wrong.
HANK. Nothing. — The flowers —
MICHAEL. — Oh, I can bring them over in the morning — you don't have to bother with them now.
HANK. No, no, you keep them. I just want Patsy and Jessica's note. It was very beautiful. They must have put a lot of thought into it. — I guess I'd forget my head if it wasn't ....

*(RICK picks up the envelope, hands it to HANK.)*

HANK. Thanks, Rick.
RICK. I'll walk you to the subway. I go your way.
HANK. — Okay. — Goodnight, Michael.
RICK. Yes, and thanks again.
MICHAEL. You're welcome, Rick. — and *bon chance*.

*(HANK smiles at RICK, puts his hand on RICK's shoulder and they go out. MICHAEL turns to survey the damage (which isn't all that bad), and exits the terrace doors.*
*For a moment, the stage is empty, then the doorbell rings. MICHAEL enters from the terrace with the stack of plates and takes them into the kitchen. The bell rings again. MICHAEL enters, turns the lights down low, crosses to the door to open it.)*

MICHAEL. *(Crestfallen.)* — Ohh, *you* again! How'd you get in *this* time?!
HAROLD. Hank and Rick were just leaving together. — Interesting.
MICHAEL. *(Deliberately.)* The ... party ... is ... over.

*(HAROLD "casually" enters. MICHAEL steps into the corridor, looks about.)*

HAROLD. Now it's so dark in here, you need night-vision glasses. — I take it you were expecting someone other than myself just now.

*(MICHAEL comes back into the room, closes the door, flips on the lights, turns to HAROLD....)*

MICHAEL. *(Ignores the remark.)* I thought I'd gotten rid of you.
HAROLD. *(Puts on dark glasses.)* I guess so. When you opened the door, your face sank like a lost cause.
MICHAEL. *(Matter-of-fact.)* I thought it might be Scott.
HAROLD. Don't fret, he'll be back. He's not through with you yet.

*(MICHAEL is annoyed, tries not to show it.)*

MICHAEL. *(Reasonably.)* I love him, Harold.
HAROLD. But he doesn't love you. He never has, and he never will no matter how much you invest in him. And that's the plain and simple truth. If you want someone, go after someone you can get.
MICHAEL. I don't *want* anyone I can get!
HAROLD. *(Offhandedly.)* — Who'd Jason leave with?
MICHAEL. Donald.
HAROLD. *Not* so interesting. But interesting.
MICHAEL. God, Jason's so common, I bet he smokes in the shower.
HAROLD. Listen, every time I look in Scott's face I think of Easter Island.
MICHAEL. *(Testily.)* When I met Scott, I knew instantly he had intelligence and potential.

HAROLD. Well, he *had* seen a movie with subtitles.

MICHAEL. I thought you were so eager to get home to that blond who was with you at the service!

HAROLD. I am. He's almost *obscenely* sexy, doncha think?

MICHAEL. *(Magnanimously.)* I'm not being judgmental about your choice of companions, Harold. You know I don't give a good goddamn about morals, but *taste* is everything! *(HAROLD sucks a tooth.)* — What're you going to do with that boy? Tonight, I mean. When you *finally* get home.

HAROLD. We *may* pull a condom over the entire apartment and have safe sex, or I *may* just take my eight-hundred-milligram Xanax and a tall beverage and isolate.

MICHAEL. Well, I hope you're careful After all, who knows about his status.

HAROLD. I know his status, and he knows mine. But maybe I'll just have to settle for chinning myself on his nipple rings.

MICHAEL. And you gave that trash the key to your apartment.

HAROLD. Scott has the key to yours, doesn't he?

MICHAEL. You can spare me any character analysis of Scott.

HAROLD. That oughta be like a dial tone.

MICHAEL. You disapprove, like Donald.

HAROLD. I don't do *anything* like Donald. — It would be too easy to call Scott a cock-teaser. It would also be unfair because I think he has *some* consideration for you in his own mixed-up, sorry way.

MICHAEL. You just think I'm a fool.

HAROLD. All you need are bells and a scepter.

MICHAEL. *(Tongue-in-cheek bravura.)* I like a *challenge*. *(Grimly.)* — He let me down about school. Again.

HAROLD. He'll let you down again and again and again. And you'll forgive him again and again and again. I think that's what love is all about.

MICHAEL. You've never let me down, Harold.

HAROLD. You never tried to put me through college.

MICHAEL. *(Short.)* What did you come back for?! — Are you still *stoned*!?
HAROLD. I wish I were, but I didn't want to blur the edges before I returned. — I wanted to be completely ... well, as you always put it — I wanted my faculties functioning at their maximum natural capacity. *(There is a more awkward pause, a silence between them as HAROLD looks directly at MICHAEL. After a moment.)* I've got AIDS. It's still with us, you know — despite the dancing in the streets. *(Reacts to MICHAEL's expression.)* — Now, don't go and get all ....
MICHAEL. *(Interrupting sharply.)* I'm not going to go and get all anything! —

*(Contrary to what he says, MICHAEL seems dazed.)*

HAROLD. Well, for god's sake, don't cry.
MICHAEL. You know I never cry in a *real* crisis.
HAROLD. *(Indirectly.)* It's the lies we tell ourselves that really matter.
MICHAEL. *(Ignores this.)* What about all the new medications?
HAROLD. It's probably a tad too late for the cocktail hour. Besides, who knows if I'm one of those who can tolerate the mix.
MICHAEL. *(Stupefied.)* — How long have you known?
HAROLD. Two months.
MICHAEL. *Two months*!
HAROLD. Yeah, I'm a tricky little thing.
MICHAEL. How do you feel? — Do you *know* how you feel?
HAROLD. *(Removes dark glasses.)* In an odd way, like Hank said, I feel relieved. I've spent a lifetime thinking about death. One thing I know I'm going to try to do: be a better Jew. And by that I don't mean run to temple every time I have an anxiety attack. What I mean is — try to practice some of the things I really believe in.
MICHAEL. Are you gonna get religion now so you can go to

heaven?

HAROLD. Not a all. Catholics are worried about what comes after — you know, carry your cross today, and go to the party later. — Jews are more focused on the here and now — business, family, food. All that kosher stuff is based on living well *now*. I'm going to try to live well in the here and now and let tomorrow take care of itself.

MICHAEL. I'm all for that. — You mean you knew when you went to St. Bart's?!

HAROLD. I didn't go to St. Bart's in the West Indies. I went to St. Vincent's in the West Village. — Well, the paramedics had to haul me away. I had pneumocystis. I had to stay for the full twenty-one days. Then home for another ....

MICHAEL. Why in the world didn't you *tell* me?! Why didn't you *call* me?

HAROLD. I *did* call you.

MICHAEL. From the *hospital*?! I thought you were calling from ....

HAROLD. — That's what I *wanted* you to think. I certainly didn't want to see anybody, and I didn't want anybody to see me. — I was too sick. — But tonight, well, I wanted you to know.

MICHAEL. *(Blankly.)* No one else knows?

HAROLD. Naturally, my doctor knows. And the odd divine, tawny attendant. — Actually, I don't care *who* knows I have AIDS, I just don't want anyone to know I'm gay.

*(He turns toward the front door.)*

MICHAEL. Where're you going?
HAROLD. Home to that heavenly creature.
MICHAEL. — Wait a minute. —
HAROLD. *(Turns back.)* Why?
MICHAEL. *(Heatedly serious.)* Oh, Harold, you can't be that

glib about mortality!
HAROLD. *(Eyeball-to-eyeball.) I* can.

*(A pause. They continue to look at each other directly....)*

MICHAEL. *(Heartfelt, quietly.)* — I'll be there for you, you know that.
HAROLD. *(Seriously.)* It never crossed my mind that you wouldn't be. *(A beat.)* — That is, if you don't perish in a private plane crash on your next junket to the Cote D'Azur. *(After a moment, with meaning.)* — I know you'll do whatever I want. Whatever it takes — fight City Hall, face the dawn with arms liked, ride a *float* even.
MICHAEL. *(Without rancor.)* Harold, I'm serious. —
HAROLD. I know you are, and that's why I can't be.
MICHAEL. *(After a moment.)* We'll get through this together.

*(HAROLD is both touched and made somewhat anxious by the genuine declaration of love for him.)*

HAROLD. *(Turns to leave.)* I really do have to go now, and I'm not just trying to get out of here — although I'm trying like hell to get out of here. *(Old brand of wryness.)* I don't want blondie to break the Lalique samovar. *(Goes, stops, turns, says genuinely.)* — I had such spilkus I just couldn't *not* not tell you any longer. I know that's a triple negative, but fuck it. — When I heard you speak at the memorial this afternoon, I knew I had come clean. — I liked what you said about Larry. — I hope you'll say a few words about me....
MICHAEL. Harold. —
HAROLD. Something like "He was a smart-ass with heart. A Scorpio with vulnerability." —

*(MICHAEL nods, refusing to give in to the moment....)*

MICHAEL. I'll think of something. *(Then, sincerely.)* I do wish you would have told me earlier.

HAROLD. I didn't want anybody there!

MICHAEL. *(Incredulously.)* You didn't want *me* there?! *Me*, of all people?!

HAROLD. Yes, you of *all* people!

MICHAEL. How can you say a thing like that about me?!

HAROLD. Now you sound like my mother!

MICHAEL. *(Sardonically.)* — By the way, tell me, is your mother still dead?

HAROLD. *(Half incensed, half amused.)* She is presently deceased, yes. — But when I'm around you, I'm not so sure! *(Hating what he's about to say.)* — You know, *nobody* can get to me the way you and my mother can! *(Corrects himself.)* — Could! *(Quickly.) Can! (Tries again.) Could ... and can*!

MICHAEL. Calm down.

HAROLD. Oh, eat shit and die!

MICHAEL. You have every right to be angry.

HAROLD. You know, I think I liked you better when you were drunk!

MICHAEL. You know what? I liked *you* better when I was drunk too!

HAROLD. *(Quickly, with "dignity.")* I also think with whatever time I have left, I oughta start hanging out with a better class of losers!

MICHAEL. *(Matching him.)* Well, you can start tonight in your own bed!

HAROLD. *(Matching him.)* At least there's somebody *in my bed tonight*!

MICHAEL. *("Grandly.")* I hate you when you get like this.

HAROLD. *(Philosophically.)* Well, you *are* what you *hate*.

MICHAEL. *(Wearily.)* Oh, Harold, let's *not*! —

HAROLD. *(Fiercely vulgar.)* No goddamit, *let's*! —

MICHAEL. *(Evenly.)* — We're too old for this game!!
HAROLD. *(Facetiously.)* Too analyzed, too grown up, too mature?!
MICHAEL. *Yes*! And too *old*!
HAROLD. *I'm* the one who's analyzed, grown up and mature! — *You're* just *old*! You peaked at eighteen and it's been downhill ever since. And you are now fifty-nine and counting!
MICHAEL. Thank you and fuck you!! *(MICHAEL quickly picks up HAROLD's rain cape and umbrella and tosses them to him.)* GETOUTTOHERE!
HAROLD. *(Exiting the apartment.)* CALLYATOMORROW!!!

*(MICHAEL slams the front door.*
*After a moment, MICHAEL turns, slowing goes to open the bar. He stands, looking at all the colored bottles and sparkling glasses.*
*As MICHAEL stands staring at the tempting display ... will he or won't he? ... Slowly, all lights fade to black.)*


**END OF THE PLAY**

## I'M NOT THE MAN I PLANNED
(From THE MEN FROM THE BOYS)

Lyrics by MART CROWLEY                Music by LARRY GROSSMAN

Music © 2002 Sunning Hill Music, Inc. & Warner-Tamerlane Music

## THE MEN FROM THE BOYS

## THE MEN FROM THE BOYS

## THE MEN FROM THE BOYS

95

## THE MEN FROM THE BOYS

**THE MEN FROM THE BOYS** 97

# THE MEN FROM THE BOYS

not in To-pe-ka any-more — And I'm not the man I planned.

## COSTUMES

The play takes place in "real time" and each character has only one costume. However, Scott changes his damp T-shirt for one of Michael's expensive sweaters.


MICHAEL: Charcoal gray business suit, charcoal tie, white shirt with
 collar and long sleeves, black belt, black shoes and sox.

DONALD: Brooks Brothers-type dark blue blazer with brass buttons,
 charcoal flannel trousers, "Ivy League" Oxford cloth pink button-
 down shirt, "Ivy League" striped rep tie (pink and navy or gold
 and navy), "penny" loafers, navy blue sox.

HANK: Dark conservative business suit (medium gray or
 herringbone), pale blue shirt with collar and long sleeves,
 conservative dark tie (medium gray or navy blue), dark shoes and
 sox, dark umbrella.

BERNARD: Navy blue suit, conservative striped shirt with collar and
 long sleeves, conservative tie (with some color), tan raincoat,
 dark shoes and sox.

EMORY. Expensive black cashmere, wool or velour jacket, black
 velour trousers, brightly colored silk bow tie, black shirt with
 collar and long sleeves, black indoor "carpet slippers," formal
 black silk sox, black shoes (for final exit), black hat (for final
 exit), black "carry-all" (for carpet slippers, jewelry and makeup).

HAROLD: Black suit, red shirt with collar and long sleeves, matching
 red ascot, black shoes, bright yellow rain cape with hood,
 umbrella, dark glasses.

## THE MEN FROM THE BOYS

RICK: Medium gray pants, dark or medium gray sweater with lighter design, light gray shirt with collar and long sleeves, dark shoes.

SCOTT: Black jeans, white T-shirt, dark shoes. Changes T-shirt at end of ACT I for an expensive, colorful cashmere sweater which belongs to Michael.

JASON: Dark pants, dark shirt or T-shirt, dark leather jacket, dark shoes or boots, dark umbrella.

## THE MEN FROM THE BOYS

## PROPERTY LIST

Preset on stage:
    Chrome and black Naugahyde armchair on marks
    Black Naugahyde sofa on marks
    Chrome coffee table on marks
        *On coffee table:*
    Cell phone
    Chrome rolling bar cart on marks
        *On bar cart:*
    Silver coffeepot (with coffee)
    1 coffee cup and saucer
    Filled champagne bottle in glass bucket (with ice)
    9 champagne flutes
    Glass ice bucket (with ice)
    Chrome étagère (bookcase)
        *On étagère:*
    1 silver frame with picture of Larry in hat on beach
    1 silver frame picture of Scott in tie and jacket
    1 cassette player
    "Hidden" bar cabinet in right wall
        *On shelves:*
    Numerous bottles of liquor, colored liqueurs, wine …
    Numerous bar glasses (for whiskey, brandy, liqueurs …)
    Corkscrew
        *Inside lower cabinet:*
    4 exterior chair seat cushions

*Preset offstage left (Kitchen)*
    Silver tray of hors d'oeuvres (edible)
    Guitar in case
    Bottle of beer

## THE MEN FROM THE BOYS

<u>Preset in Bedroom — Second level</u>
    Chrome chair on marks
    Bed (specially made) with cover on marks
    Bedside table on marks

<u>Props preset offstage — Second level</u>
    *In bathroom:*
    2 towels (for Donald)
    Michael's expensive sweater (for Scott)
    Emory's carry-all bag
    Emory's makeup and jewelry
    Emory's red ostrich fan
    Emory's street shoes
    Emory's hat
    Bernard's raincoat
    Hank's umbrella

<u>Personal Props:</u>
    Emory's embroidery (needle, yarn and pattern)
    Emory's song cassette (piano accompaniment)
    Michael's wallet containing several bills

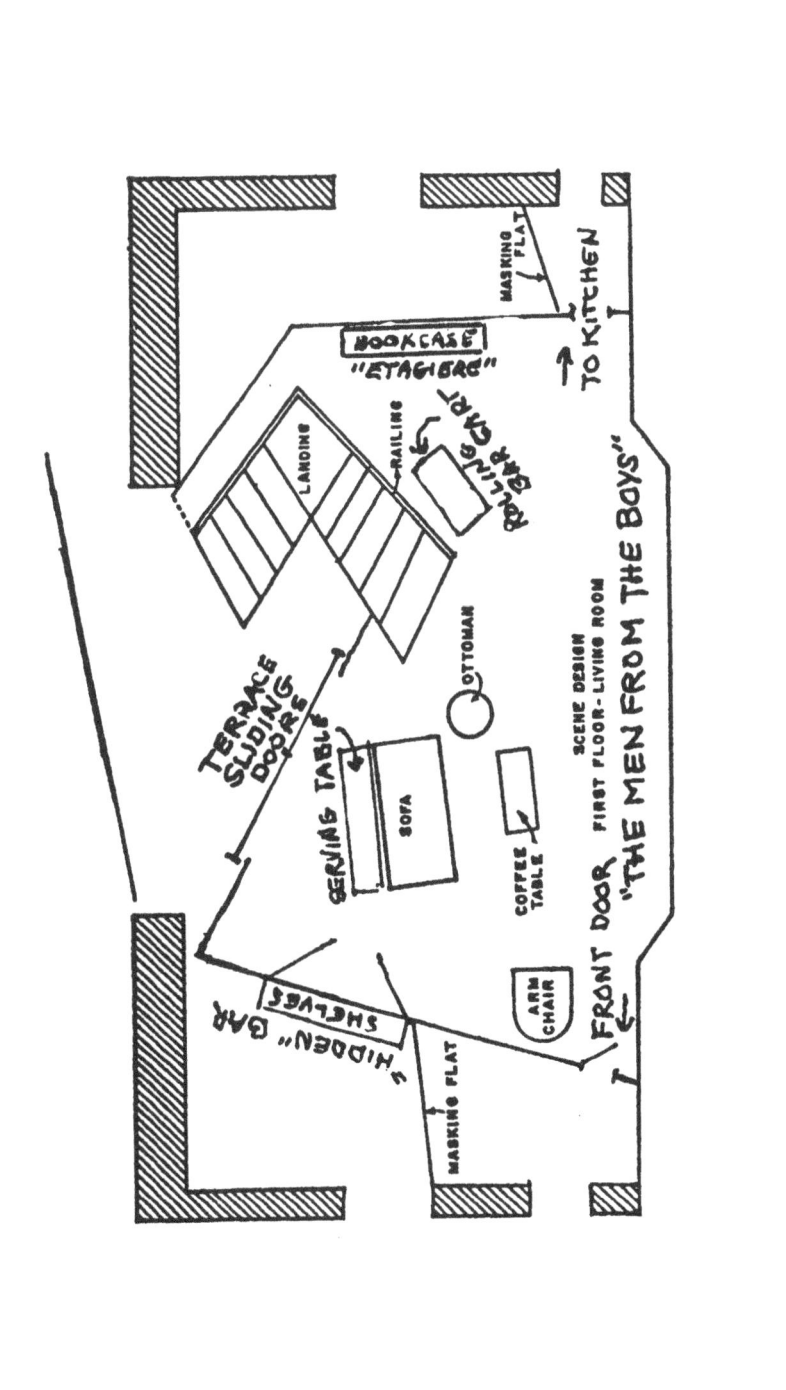

SCENE DESIGN  FIRST FLOOR–LIVING ROOM
"THE MEN FROM THE BOYS"

SCENE DESIGN
SECOND FLOOR - BEDROOM

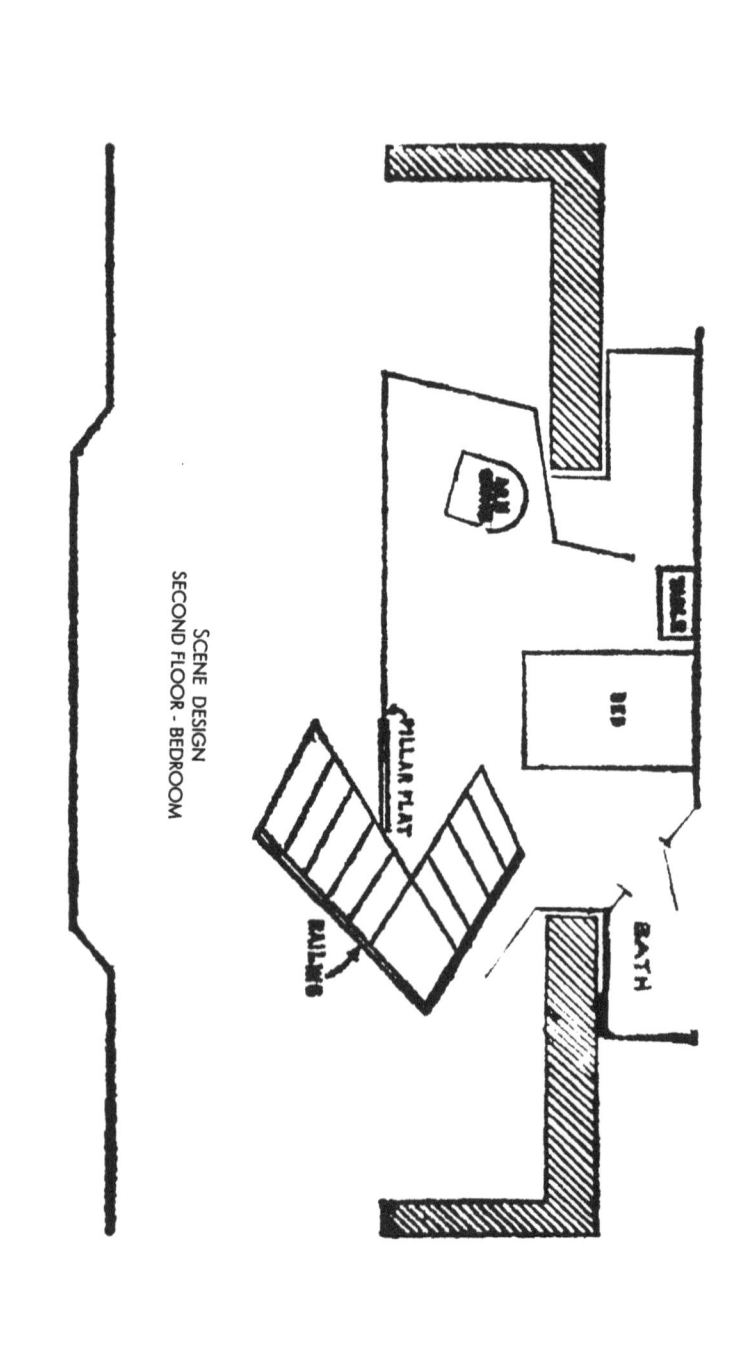

Milton Keynes UK
Ingram Content Group UK Ltd.
UKHW030210111224
452348UK00012B/922